COLTER SONS BOOK 6

THE RESILIENT BRIDE

Karen Baney

desert life
media

The Resilient Bride: Colter Sons Book 6
By Karen Baney

Publisher:
Desert Life Media, LLC
Gilbert, AZ 85295

www.karenbaney.com

Printed in the United States of America

ISBN 979-8-9863369-7-8

When the righteous cry for help, the Lord hears and delivers them out of all their troubles. The Lord is near to the brokenhearted and saves the crushed in spirit.
—Psalm 34:17-18

CHAPTER I

Prescott, Arizona Territory
April 14, 1906

VIOLET

I was unlucky in love. After three attempts at marriage, all I had to show for my efforts was a toddler son and a casket lowering my beloved Forest into the ground.

My first attempt came when I was nineteen. I fell hard for Andrew Ward, and he fell hard for me. At least that was what I thought until the moment when I stood outside the church in my wedding dress as I held onto my papa's arm, waiting for the music to start. I was supposed to walk down the aisle and promise my life to Andrew Ward. Only he never showed. Instead, he ran off with Catherine Parker the night before. They married down in Wickenburg without telling me that...

Well, he told me nothing. Not that he wouldn't marry me or that he didn't love me. Certainly not that he really loved Catherine. Instead, the scoundrel left me standing outside of the church in my wedding dress believing that I was about to experience the best day of my life while he up and married my friend. While I waited for the humiliation and rejection to fade, I moved back home with my parents at the ranch.

Then I met Cooper James. Ah, those flashing green eyes and charming smile that could melt the ice off the coldest heart. Our courtship was fast; just a few months. He proposed in June 1900. We set a wedding date for the first weekend in August. Then we bought a house in town. Eager to begin my new life with my new love, I started furnishing our house long before our wedding day.

But then the strangest thing happened. The night of the great fire, July 14, 1900, the entire business district of the town burnt down. It was the last time anyone talked to Cooper. Some people thought he helped fight the fire, but no one saw him the next day. No one died in that fire. They found no bodies. Not his. Not anyone's. Oddly, his horse was gone, too. His bank account cleaned out. There was no note. No word. No information. And no wedding. He vanished without a trace.

So, by the time I met Forest Gamble, I was twice stood up. I made him work hard to win my heart, having learned my lesson twice over. But, slowly over time, Forest won my heart through a long courtship. I finally agreed to a wedding date. The months leading up to our wedding, Forest reassured me many times that he'd show up and he spoke the truth when he said he wanted to spend the rest of his life with me. Despite my fears, my wedding day came. He was there with his kind brown eyes full of love for me. Papa walked me down the aisle and I promised my heart and soul to my husband.

Forest kept his word, and we shared many wonderful years together. I loved him. He loved me. Our son, Will, was evidence of our love. We were a family. Unfortunately, the rest of Forest's life only lasted four years.

God had some strange sense of humor, I thought, as the first pile of dirt dropped onto Forest's casket in the ground. I sniffed as the numbness swallowed my heart. Will tugged on my arm. As Mama took his other hand, I let go. At twenty-seven, I became a widow and the single mother of a toddler. My husband would shortly be six feet under. Gone. Forever apart from me.

My heart died that day and I didn't plan on ever unearthing it again. It would not withstand another significant loss.

After I straightened my shoulders and climbed into the carriage, I wiped away the lone tear that trickled down my cheek. Mama handed Will to me, and I held him close. My childhood friend Keri sat next to her husband, my oldest brother, James. He clucked the horses into motion.

When we arrived at James's house, he helped Keri down. Then he took Will from me and helped me down. Keri opened the front door to their extravagant mansion as their children greeted them loudly.

I retreated to the parlor when the nanny took Will for a nap. It was quiet. It would be for a short time before the mourners came to express their sympathies.

Don't misunderstand me. I appreciated the love and support from family and friends. I was grateful that James and Keri opened their home to me for a few days. Soon enough, I would return to my home. The home that was mine and Forest's. It was mine alone now.

I had a conversation with God before the mourners arrived. *Why did you take my husband? Why put me through heartbreak after heartbreak?* I wanted my husband back, but he was gone. I would never allow myself to fall in love again. Ever.

As I looked out the window, Mama slid an arm around my waist. She said nothing. Just her presence comforted me.

When mourners filled the room, I sat near the fireplace. Forest was well-loved by his co-workers at the bank. No one could believe he was really gone. What a tragic thing. Such a strange accident. It was so senseless. Or so they told me.

Oddly, his passing made complete sense to me. God didn't want me to be married. Clearly. So, I was done with love. I would support my son. My brothers were the male influences he would need in the years to come. James already doted on him. Boone loved him as much as his own children. Grady, well, he wasn't a blood brother to me, but he was as close as any of my actual brothers. He thought the world of Will.

Somehow, I would find a way forward. I would be just fine without a man in my home. I could do it.

As the crowd thinned, I climbed the stairs and fell into the guest bed upstairs. I didn't bother to take off the black widow's gown or let my hair down. I just flopped down on it and closed my eyes.

I imagined Forest by my side. Though he'd been gone only a few days, I missed him terribly.

Exhaustion pulled at me. Somehow, I would move forward. Alone.

CHAPTER 2

Prescott, Arizona Territory
June 29, 1906

ZAYNE

Eleanor Grace fussed in my arms. As I shifted my nine-month-old daughter to lean against my chest, I hoped she didn't need changed. One thing I learned on the long train ride from Tucson: the world was not helpful nor kind to a single father traveling with his infant daughter.

Believe me, I would have much rather been traveling with my wife. Better yet, I would have preferred to stay in Tucson with Rose. But my desires and wants did not matter. Eleanor was with me. Rose was not. She had made the greatest sacrifice a mother could make for her unborn child. She gave up her life to bring Eleanor into this world.

As Eleanor fussed again, I sighed and dug around in my satchel, which was stuffed full of things for my daughter. Surely, I had one bottle left. When she let loose a full-blown wail, I moved her to one arm. At last, my fingers wrapped around the bottle. I grabbed it and jammed it in her mouth. Relief washed over me as she sucked on it and calmed.

I was totally ill-equipped to be a single father. Even after nine months, I didn't know what I was doing. I mean, I had worked out a system, mostly because of the graciousness of the wet nurse that provided for Eleanor in the earliest days of her life.

As soon as she was weaned and became my responsibility alone, I knew I was in over my head. My work suffered so much so that my older brother, Martin, moved down to Tucson to take over managing the freight office.

After a few months, we struck a deal. He moved his family to Tucson to run the Tucson office, and I would move home with Mama. Then I was to replace him at the Prescott office. He told me Mama was eager to help with Eleanor.

So, I finally boarded the train headed for Prescott with my daughter.

"She's so sweet," the woman in the seat next to me said.

I held back a snort. Eleanor had been anything but sweet on the train. Fussy. Cranky. Stinky. But not sweet.

"Are you headed to Prescott?" she asked.

"Yes."

"Oh, you must stop at the pie shop in the station. Vi makes the best pies. Any kind of pie you can imagine, even savory pie. The crust. It's so fluffy. Best pie I've ever had."

I gave the woman a wan smile as I laid a cloth over my shoulder and burped my daughter. The woman kept talking about pies until I craved some.

At last, the train arrived at the Prescott station. I stepped aside to allow the talkative woman to exit. Then I waited for the initial rush of passengers to clear out before I laid Eleanor on a seat. I gathered my satchel and another bag, which I slung over one shoulder. Then I picked her up again and exited the train.

I glanced around the platform for my brother, Loren, and

my mother. I didn't spot either of them, so I followed the aroma of fresh baked pie.

"Vi's Pies," I muttered under my breath as I dropped my heavy bags on a chair.

Eleanor fussed, then wailed, before an unpleasant odor wafted up to greet me. She needed changed.

"Couldn't you wait until Mama was here?" I pleaded with her.

Of course, the deed was already done. I sighed. Then I contemplated the idea of changing her right there on the pie shop's table. I quickly discarded the idea. I certainly didn't want to eat on a table where a baby's diaper had just been.

I bounced her up and down trying to calm her, which only made the smell worse.

"Need help?" The chatty woman from the train asked.

"Yes. She needs changed and, well, I'm not sure what to do."

She quirked an eyebrow.

"I mean, I know what to do, just not where."

"Let me take her to the facilities. There is a place there. I'll be back right away."

I hesitated. I didn't really know the woman.

"That's alright. My mother should be here shortly. It can wait."

She shrugged and walked away.

As I flopped down onto the chair, I resigned myself to wait for my mother.

My stomach growled, and I looked longingly at the case of pies. Cherry. Apple. Pecan. Several others that I couldn't determine what they were.

A young woman with dark hair and brilliant blue eyes stood behind the counter. Those eyes. I'd recognize them anywhere. My heart nearly stopped beating as I studied her. She wore a black dress with a stark white apron. She smiled sweetly at the chatty woman from the train, though the smile didn't quite reflect in her eyes. After all this time, her beauty still captivated me.

When the chatty woman finished, I stepped forward.

"Violet Colter?" I asked. My heart pounded against my rib cage, as if it tried to escape my chest.

When she looked up from the till, she smiled brightly until her gaze connected with mine. Then a frown shadowed her face. A few seconds later, a forced smile graced her lips.

"Zayne Harrison." Her voice sounded overly bright. "It's Gamble now."

"What's Gamble?"

"My name. Mrs. Forest Gamble."

I let out a nervous laugh. "My apologies."

She sniffed and nodded to Eleanor. "I think she needs a fresh diaper."

Heat warmed my face. "Yeah, I know. Just no place for... Um, for me to change her."

"Where's her mother?"

I cleared my throat and glanced away as my eyes stung and my throat worked. The words wouldn't move past my lips.

"Oh. I see. Here," she said as she rounded the corner of the counter. "Let me take her. Do you have an extra diaper?"

I nodded and walked toward my things. After I handed her the clean diaper, I reluctantly released my daughter into the arms of my childhood crush. My throat constricted as I watched her walk away with my baby girl.

It had been a decade since I had seen Violet Colter. Gamble. Whatever. I didn't know her now. I worried if I could trust her with Eleanor.

No matter. It was too late. I was at her mercy.

A woman stepped up to the counter. "Can I help you, sir?"

I glanced the direction that Violet took before I answered. "I'll take a slice of apple pie. Wait, make that two."

After I dropped some coins into her waiting palm, she placed the money in the cash register. Then she dished up two slices of pie on two separate plates and handed them to me with two forks. I didn't have the heart to tell her I planned on eating them both.

As I walked back to the table, Violet approached with Eleanor. "I hope you don't mind, but I tossed the soiled diaper in the trash bin outside."

"That's fine. I have plenty more in my luggage." Truthfully, I was relieved. It was the best way to handle a dirty diaper while traveling.

I held my arms out for Eleanor, but Violet shook her head. "Enjoy your pie. I'll hold her for a few minutes."

My eyes followed her every movement while I stuffed large bites of pie in my mouth. She paced near the table, bouncing Eleanor on one hip. She seemed perfectly at ease with a baby in her arms. My heart skipped a beat, and I scolded myself. I didn't move home to reconnect with a woman from my past. I was there to raise my daughter with Mama's help and focus on my job.

As Violet sat across from me, she smiled. It seemed genuine that time. "What brings you to Prescott? Last I heard, you lived in Tucson."

I swallowed a bite of the pie. It really had the fluffiest crust. "This is good."

Pink colored her cheeks. "Thank you. Mama taught me well."

"A pie shop, huh? How does your husband feel about your business?"

Tears pooled in her eyes. Idiot. She wore a black dress, a

mourning dress. Not a uniform.

She cleared her throat. "I think he would have been proud I figured out how to provide for myself and our son."

Son. She had a boy. I wondered how old he was, but decided I'd already stuck my foot in my mouth once. I'd much rather stick another bite of pie in it.

When I cleaned the first plate, I pushed it away and slid the second one in front of me.

"Oh, that's for you?" she teased. "I thought maybe it was for me."

She winked after a few seconds.

"If you'd like a piece, I'll be happy to buy you one."

"No need. I know the owner. She gives me free pie for life."

For the first time in a year, I laughed out loud from a place I'd forgotten existed.

"Sorry for your loss," I said, before eating another bite.

"As I am for you. I suppose this sweetie is the reason you're here?" She looked down at my daughter and lightly brushed her slender fingers on Eleanor's belly. She smiled and whispered words to her eliciting a cheeky smile from my girl.

My heart ached as I pictured Rose doing the same. Only Rose wasn't there.

"Yes. Mama is going to help raise her."

"How is your mother? I heard your father passed a few years ago."

"Nine years ago now," I said, failing to keep the sadness from my voice. At twenty-eight, I lost more family than most. I missed my papa more than I cared to admit out loud.

"Really? I hadn't realized it's been that long."

"She remarried. Jedediah Cole is her new husband. He is in finance. Works for the railroad."

Her eyes lit up. "Oh, James probably works with him."

I nodded. Then I held out my hands for Eleanor.

Violet sighed as she relinquished my daughter. "I do miss holding babies."

"Thank you for your help, Violet."

"Zayne!" My mama's voice drew my attention. "There you are!"

I stood and waved to my mother. When I glanced back over my shoulder, Violet was gone. So were the two empty pie plates. It bothered me she had hurried away without a farewell.

Mama pulled me into her arms and hugged me loosely, careful not to squish her granddaughter.

"Oh, she's so beautiful. Just like Rose."

I coughed as the comparison hit the core of my heart. I thought the same many times, but to hear it out loud hurt deeper than I expected.

Loren greeted me as Mama took Eleanor. "Where are your things?"

"I couldn't really manage them and her, so I figured we could collect them once you were here."

He nodded as I picked up my satchel and other things from the table. I glanced over my shoulder and caught Violet looking my way. I waved a hand before I turned and headed toward the freight docks.

CHAPTER 3

VIOLET

Zayne Harrison was back in town. I frowned. Zayne, the boy who played dozens of pranks on me. Frogs in my lunch pail. Ripped pages from my primer. A harmless snake in the sleeve of my coat. My brothers used to tease me and tell me it meant Zayne liked me. If that was true, the feeling wasn't mutual. I despised Zayne Harrison.

Until I saw him with his daughter in his arms. He looked lost and frazzled. I had never traveled with Will as a baby. Not any further than a church or store. When he was small, I never even went to the ranch. I could not imagine a train ride from Tucson with a baby, and I understood why he looked worn out.

My compassionate nature won as I changed his daughter's diaper. When I returned to the table, I sensed his eyes on me while I held his daughter. With a fresh diaper, she smelled sweet again. Her soft skin made me long for another baby.

Once I handed her back to him, I recognized the gratitude in his soft blue-gray eyes. It felt good to help someone else.

When he asked me about Forest, my heart split in two. It shocked me Zayne Harrison cared.

I shook my head as I walked back to the kitchen.

Then I smiled. He bought two slices of pie and he enjoyed every bite.

That was why I opened a pie shop. Pie made people happy. It brought nostalgic feelings and memories of holidays or special events. It comforted a person after a taxing day. Pie delivered a dose of cheer for even the most weary, snippy passenger.

And I loved baking pies. I loved thinking up new recipes. Most of all, I enjoyed the effect pie had on my customers. It was the perfect job for me.

When I pitched the idea to James, he didn't hesitate for one second. He asked how much money I needed to start it and then he promised if it wasn't enough, he would provide more. Whatever I needed, he had said.

He reminded me that my pies rivaled Mama's and Mama was the best pie baker in the county. She won the prize at several fairs. The only one who beat her pies in recent years was me and my original creations. Mama didn't mind in the least. She was proud of me.

When I told her about my plans, her only words were, "Of course you are opening a pie shop." It was as if she already knew I would do it.

"Aunt Vi!" My nephew Sterling called my name from the front counter.

"Just a minute!" I replied as I placed a few pies in the oven. I set a timer before I went out to meet him.

Will squirmed from Sterling's shoulders, so he placed my son back on the ground. I crouched down and opened my arms for Will. He giggled and launched himself against me.

"How was your trip to the ranch?" I asked my two-and-a-half-year-old.

"Ster horse."

I smiled. "Ster" was all Will managed of his much older

cousin's name.

"Is that so? Did the horse go fast?"

Will giggled. "Fast!"

I glanced at Sterling. He shook his head. "Nothing more than a trot."

I nodded my approval. Then I stood and hugged Sterling. "Thank your parents for me for watching him the last few days."

"Mama said any time. I think Grandma would keep him forever if he didn't require so much energy."

"How is Papa doing?"

Sterling glanced away. "Well enough, I suppose. Grandma says his arthritis has been acting up something fierce lately. Though they still walk over for supper every evening."

"You are a good grandson and a good man."

"Thanks, Vi. Mama asked when you might come out for a visit."

I sighed. "With the new pie shop, I only have Sundays off. Maybe when I settle into a routine. Things are still too new."

When he walked away, I smiled full of pride. Sam and El-lie Mae had raised such a fine young man. Recently, he had taken over some responsibilities from his father. He was so good with Will, too. Always so patient.

"I'll clean up if you want to head home," my employee, Katie volunteered.

Katie Noble just turned eighteen and begged her father to let her have a job. Her father worked with my brother, James, at the Santa Fe, Prescott, & Phoenix Railway, so when he heard about my venture he allowed her to apply. Her pleasing personality and smile endeared her to me. She learned the duties of the front counter immediately. She had more to learn before she would bake pies on her own, but she always maintained a positive attitude.

"Thank you, Katie. Come on, Will, let's go home."

"Home," he giggled.

When I reached for him, he ran away from my grasp and made a game out of it. After two laps around the worktable in the kitchen, Katie helped me corral him. Then I lifted him up and settled him against my side. He squirmed, but I wasn't comfortable allowing him to cross the street while holding my hand because he often pulled out of my grip.

I carried him for a few more blocks until we turned onto a quiet street. Then I set him down and held his hand as we walked the last block to our home.

When I opened the door, a pang of nostalgia hit me. Forest had been gone for over two months. Many times, I daydreamed that he sat at the table, waiting for me. He'd be sipping a coffee while reading the paper. Perhaps one day the longing would fade.

After I closed the door of the house, I released Will's hand. He ran to his toy blocks and started building a structure that kept his attention. He was used to our new routine at last. Play time while I freshened up and cooked supper.

I entered our bedroom. My bedroom. My eyes burned, and I blinked rapidly. I wondered how long it would be before I could enter the room or crawl into bed at night without thinking of Forest and the warmth of his body next to mine as his soft breathing calmed me.

As I removed my mourning gown, I took a deep breath. I must stop torturing myself with such memories. After I splashed some cool water on my face, I blotted it dry with a soft towel. Then I donned a simple, comfortable work dress. I frowned when I noticed it seemed a little snugger around my midsection. Odd. I was not eating enough. Perhaps I ate more than I realized.

I pushed the thought aside and returned to the main room

of our house. The large kitchen opened up to the dining room and living room. Our bedroom ran the length of one side of the upstairs. Will's bedroom and an empty room were on the other side. Even though we hoped to make it a nursery for a baby, none came.

I remembered a conversation with Forest about children.

"What if we have more than two?" I asked.

He laughed. "I hope we do. When that time comes, I will be settled in my career at the bank. I will buy you a larger home."

A larger home. Just one of the many dreams I shared with my husband that would remain unfulfilled. A tear ran down my face. I wiped it with the back of my hand.

Then I started a fire in the stove and cooked a simple meal. Someday, I would put a roast in the oven at lunch. Until then, I only had the energy for cooking on the stovetop.

James suggested more than once that I hire help. Someone who could cook and clean and help with Will. I reminded him I was a widow and didn't have deep pockets or funds like he earned at the railroad. He offered to pay for it all.

I sighed as I stirred the fried potatoes. I had already accepted far too much of his charity. After Cooper's disappearance, I lived with him and Keri for a while, until I married Forest. Since Forest's passing, James paid for the rent at the pie shop and the cost to start up the business. He took no percentage of the profits. Instead, he insisted that I not worry about paying him back and that it was his pleasure to help me.

As I retrieved plates from the cupboard, I thought about my strange relationship with James. He was the oldest of us Colter children. I was the surprise baby, the youngest that came eight years after my closest sibling. James and I were thirteen years apart. My mother had my five brothers in six years' time. A few of my brothers were barely a year apart.

By the time I was old enough to remember my siblings, James moved out and worked as a railroad man in Tucson, then in Prescott. He only came home to visit a few times a year, like for his birthday or holidays, if he wasn't traveling. When I was a teenager, he married, and we saw more of him.

I think my childhood friendship with Keri played a part in his eagerness to help me. Whenever I asked, he always said he was glad to help me. That's what family did.

The smell of burned food pulled me from my thoughts. I quickly removed the potatoes from the stove. Only a few small pieces were burnt. After I set the pan on a towel, I grabbed the plates I had set aside earlier. Three. I sighed as I placed the extra one back in the cupboard.

Someday I would remember I was alone. Just me and Will. That Forest was truly gone and never coming back.

"Will, supper is ready."

"Papa."

My lungs squeezed all the air out. My chest tightened at the familiar name my son used. I didn't know how to tell him that his papa was gone and never coming back.

"Come, eat."

"Papa."

My hands shook as the tears blurred my vision. How would I ever learn to forget my husband if my son couldn't either?

I took a deep breath and walked over to where he played with his blocks. Without a word, I lifted him into my arms and carried him to the table. I set his plate of food in front of him. When I bowed my head, I silently thanked God for the kindness and help of my family and for the provision of food on the table. After I finished, I raised my head as Will grabbed a fist full of potatoes and stuffed them in his mouth.

As exhaustion washed over me, I picked at my food. I was

weary. Weary of trying to be strong. Weary of feeling so utterly alone. It was difficult to figure out how to navigate this new life without Forest.

CHAPTER 4

ZAYNE

Loren pulled a wagon up to the freight dock of the train depot. With our connections through our late-father's freight-ing company, I shipped my belongings at the lower freight rates. It still cost me a fair amount to ship everything.

A smarter choice would have been to wire the funds to my mother to purchase a new bassinet, crib, and rocking chair. But Rose and I had picked out the furniture together. I wanted to keep them forever and pass them down to Eleanor when she was older. I wanted her to have some things from her mother. The mother that loved her more than life itself.

I shook off the gloomy thought and began loading the wagon. A large, beefy man joined us.

"Zayne, this is Smalley Junior. His father used to work with ours at the freighting company. Now he works for us."

I shook Smalley Junior's hand.

"Just call me Smalley."

"Thanks for helping," I said.

"No trouble at all." He winked at me. "I wanted to get on my boss's good side from the start."

Then he and Loren lifted the crib into the wagon. I set the rocker next to it. Then Smalley placed the bassinet next to it.

We loaded trunk after trunk into the wagon until we cleared the platform of my things.

"How much stuff did you bring?" Loren asked.

"I sold most of my possessions," I admitted. And I, at long last, donated all of Rose's clothing to the church mission after holding on to them for nearly nine months. If I hadn't moved home, I would have put it off longer.

"I think I'll stop by Hugh and Noah's shop to see if one or both of them can help," Loren said. "Allan is out on a survey trip. Otherwise, I'm sure he would have helped, too."

"I'll drive the wagon," Smalley volunteered.

I took Eleanor from Mama before Smalley helped her up to the wagon seat. She reached for her, but I shook my head. I had left the baby carriage out of the wagon so I could walk her home.

"I'll be along shortly."

Smalley started the wagon into motion as I laid Eleanor in the carriage. I strolled down the side street towards my childhood home. I had forgotten that it sat atop a hill and almost wished I would have ridden in the wagon by the time we crested it.

The sun warmed my back. Perspiration dotted my forehead. The temperature had warmed considerably since we arrived that morning. It would be fun to unload the wagon.

As soon as the house came into view, my sisters swarmed me.

"We came to help," Alice, the second oldest, said.

As Pearl pulled the carriage from my hands, she said, "Here, let me take Eleanor. Oh, isn't she just adorable?"

"Let me see," Beulah said.

Victoria, the oldest, held the door open. She was my father's first adopted child from before he met my mother. We were seventeen years apart in age. She was more like an aunt than a sister.

"There's a pitcher with water on the table in the kitchen. Please help yourself while we fuss over our niece." She smiled warmly.

I nodded my thanks as my remaining sisters, Cora, Mabel, and Wilma, crowded around the carriage. My sisters couldn't see Eleanor at the same time. But they tried anyway.

I stood there for a moment, glad and relieved to be home. Eleanor wouldn't want for love, it was certain. Not if my sisters had anything to say about it.

A smile rested on my lips as I entered the kitchen and poured myself a glass of water. I downed it and mentally prepared myself for hauling all our stuff up a flight of stairs.

As she entered the room, Mama told me the nursery should be the room at the end of the hall. "The staff can help if she stirs at night."

"I'll take care of her if she wakes up at night."

Mama frowned. "You don't need to worry about that, son. We'll take care of her."

"I'll be right there next to her. No need to bother anyone else."

Mama cleared her throat. "I set you up in the room next to her."

"That won't do. She's not old enough for me to leave her alone yet." My voice sounded defensive and stern. I ought to apologize, but I wanted one thing clear upfront. Eleanor was my child and my responsibility. I would direct her care, even though I accepted the help of others.

"I... I'm sorry. I just thought..."

Then I closed my eyes and took a deep breath before I opened them. "Thank you, Mama. I appreciate your thoughtfulness," I whispered. "I'm just not ready to sleep in separate quarters yet."

"I understand. When your brothers get here, we can move your dresser and bed into her room."

"No. Just move her things into my room. It's the one us boys shared, right?"

She nodded.

"It is bigger than the one at the end of the hall."

"Alright," she said. "I'll tell them."

When I stepped closer to Mama, I pulled her into my arms for a few seconds before releasing her. "Thank you for everything."

Her voice was thick with emotion when she spoke. "You look exactly like him."

Papa. He would have loved Eleanor just like he had loved every child that had the privilege of calling our house their home. Seven adopted daughters. Six adopted sons. And me, his only natural born child and the youngest.

"You still miss him?" I asked, confused. She remarried eight or nine years ago.

"Of course."

Her confession hit me squarely in my chest. I just assumed that in time I would forget Rose. That the memory of her would fade. I thought I'd never miss her again when I moved on.

"Your father was my first love. We shared twenty-five years together. We raised you children together. Our love was fiercely deep, Zayne. I could no more forget Joshua than I could forget my arm."

"But what about Jedediah?"

"Oh, I love Jedediah too. With all my heart." She shook her head, and I noticed for the first time how much gray graced the edges of her blond hair. "It's hard to explain. One day you'll understand there is room in your heart for both the woman you lost and the new woman you will come to love."

I snorted. "I doubt I will ever love again."

She reached up and patted my cheek. "I believe you will. You are still very young. You'll see."

She straightened her back. "Let's get the cavalry of Harrisons organized so we can move you in."

I laughed at her choice of the cavalry. Papa called us that so many times, a carryover from his days in the cavalry before he met Mama and before he started our freighting business.

When I entered the noisy parlor, I smiled. Both Hugh and Noah came. It was practically a family reunion. Only three of my brothers were not there. Martin remained in Tucson to take over for me at the freight company. Henry lived in Phoenix and managed our largest freight office. And as Loren mentioned, Allan traveled for his job as a surveyor.

That left us with eleven Harrison siblings and Smalley. We unloaded the wagon quickly while Mama watched Eleanor. As soon as everything was in my room, Beulah, Mabel, and Cora shooed me out and told me they would unpack my things. I felt a little awkward that my older sisters would handle my things. They were all married with children of their own. But it still felt weird.

None of that mattered. They pushed me out the door and gave me no choice. I gave in. It was how they showed me love. They liked to do things for me. If I wasn't happy with how they organized things, I would just reorganize it after they left.

"Are you sure you want Eleanor in with you?" Pearl asked as she passed me on the stairs.

"Absolutely."

"Alright."

When I entered the parlor again, Loren said his goodbyes. "I've reserved several tables for the Harrison clan at the Independence Day celebration. You can catch up with us then."

I nodded and thought his plan smart. Our family was too large to have a reunion at our house, especially since everyone was married with a few children. There were also Jedediah's children and grandchildren. We were probably around fifty people when we were all together.

"Martin and Henry are bringing their families up for a few days," Hugh said. "So it will be everyone."

"Looking forward to it. Thanks for your help, Hugh, Noah, Smalley."

After they left, I found Mama in her room, cooing softly to Eleanor. She looked up and held a finger to her lips. Then she whispered, "She's sleeping."

"Shall I bring the bassinet in?" I asked.

She shook her head. "I'd like to hold my granddaughter for a bit, if you don't mind."

While I leaned against the doorjamb, I listened as Mama sang softly to my daughter. My heart melted at the sight. Then a wave of sorrow overwhelmed me. It should be Rose singing over her.

The flood of grief nearly flattened me. I tried to regain control to no avail. Instead, I ran to the back porch. After I sat down, I held my head in my hands. A year's worth of pent-up grief spilled out of my soul.

My sweet Rose was gone. The ache felt as raw as the day she died. I had spent the last nine months powering through. Just trying to survive. The only thing I did well was love my daughter. I hoped to make up for her loss.

Tears and anguish bombarded me. I wasn't sure how long I had sat there. The sun lowered in the sky by the time Mama joined me.

When she said nothing and wrapped her arms around me, my tears flowed again.

"Shh. Shh." She whispered as she rocked me back and

forth. "You're here now. You and Eleanor are not alone. We will help you get through this."

I broke away from her hold, and I wiped my hand over my eyes. Then I snorted. "I do not know what came over me."

"It's called grief, Zayne. You needed to do that for some time now."

"Where's Eleanor?"

"Sleeping in a second bassinet in the kitchen. Our cook is watching her while she makes supper."

"I should go…"

When I started to stand, Mama's hand clamped down on my arm. "Sit. Rest for a bit."

Then she handed me a lemonade. "I'll warn you I made this." She laughed.

I raised an eyebrow. Then I took a long swig.

According to Papa, Mama had been a terrible cook in the early days of their marriage. Of course, she grew up in a household with a hired cook. Over the years, she became an accomplished cook, but the family still joked about her cooking skills. It was a Harrison family tradition.

"It's good," I said.

She laughed. "I know."

Then she stood and took my empty glass. "Supper will be ready in a few minutes. Jedediah is already home, so we'll eat as soon as it is ready."

Mama squeezed my shoulder. "I'm glad you're home, son, and that we can help."

"Thank you, Mama."

CHAPTER 5

ZAYNE

Two days later, I still felt like a stranger in my childhood home. The first night, Eleanor fussed often throughout the night in the strange room. I only got a few hours of sleep, much like when she was first born. Last night was better. She slept for longer stretches of several hours. I had hoped that by the time night rolled around, she would settle into a routine again.

As sunlight leaked through the edges of the closed curtains, I threw back the covers and walked over to the window. Then I opened the curtains and let the light fill the room.

"Morning, sweet girl," I whispered as I rubbed Eleanor's belly while she laid in her crib.

She coughed, then started cooing. I lifted her into my arms and held her close.

"How do you like our new home?"

She gurgled in response.

"I see. Ready to see if Grandma is awake?"

The nonsensical words that escaped her lips brought a smile to my face. I padded downstairs in my pajamas. When I entered the kitchen, the cook greeted me.

"Morning, Mr. Harrison."

"Morning, Miss Vera."

"How'd the little one sleep last night?"

"Just fine."

I took a seat and bounced Eleanor on my leg. Vera set a cup of black coffee in front of me. "Got any sugar?"

"'Course, Mr. Harrison," she said as she brought a spoon and the sugar bowl.

I dumped one teaspoon into the coffee and stirred. I never had been one for unsweetened coffee. A little sugar took the edge off the bitter liquid.

As I set the spoon aside, Mama entered the kitchen dressed in her Sunday best. "Oh, good, you're up. I was trying to decide if I should wake you."

"What time is it?" I asked as I sipped the coffee.

She came around the table and took Eleanor from me. "Almost nine."

"Oh. So sorry. I didn't realize I overslept."

"Not to worry," Mama said. "I sent Miss Harmony up to gather Eleanor's things while you eat. We'll get her ready for church while you dress."

Miss Vera set a full plate of food in front of me. I ate as quickly as I dared. Then I dashed up the stairs. I passed Miss Harmony in the hall and thanked her for taking care of Eleanor. Mama's original plan to put Eleanor in her own room may have made more sense after all.

Quickly, I undressed and splashed water over me. I glanced at the clock in my room. Not enough time to shave. Well, I was a single father. Hopefully, the church parishioners would not judge me too harshly for showing up a little scruffy.

To compensate, I donned my nicest black suit and a rich plum necktie. I buttoned the suit jacket, then I tied my shoes before I hurried downstairs.

Mama placed Eleanor in the carriage and hung the bag with diapers and bottles over the carriage handles. Then Jedediah held out his arm for her. She placed her hand in the crook of his arm.

My heart snagged. I was still adjusting to seeing Mama on another man's arm. I was not able to attend their wedding as Rose was recovering from one of her many miscarriages. Nor had I come back for a visit for several years. The only time I saw Jedediah was when he and Mama came down to Tucson to visit for a few days.

I shook off the strange feeling and pushed the carriage out the door. Then I carried it down the porch stairs before I set it back on the ground.

"Your hat, Mr. Harrison!" Harmony called after me and handed me one that matched my suit.

"Thank you," I called over my shoulder as I hurried to catch up with Mama and Jedediah. They spoke in soft tones to each other, so I lagged to give them some privacy.

By the time we arrived at church, the opening notes of the first song rang out. I knew how much Mama disliked being late. So had Papa.

I snorted under my breath. Having a baby made punctuality nearly impossible, at least when one was on his own to care for her.

When I set down the bag, it echoed in the quiet as the music had stopped. My face heated as the next song began. Eleanor slept peacefully through the singing. However, my angel became a loud, angry baby the moment the pastor stood and started his message.

"Sorry," I whispered under my breath as I lifted her into my arms.

Three of my sisters stood. I shook my head. Eleanor was

mine. I would care for her. By the time I walked to the back of the church, I was certain every eye glared at me.

"Zayne," Beulah whispered as she handed me the bag.

I flashed her a wan smile before I exited through the thick wooden doors.

Once outside, Eleanor continued to scream. I checked her diaper, and she was fine. I offered her a bottle. She refused it. That was the end of my list of things to help her stop. Unfortunately, she continued to wail.

I hugged her close and bounced her up and down as I paced back and forth across the churchyard. When the doors creaked, I glanced up in time to see Violet Colter—er Gamble—exit the church and throw up as she leaned over the railing. Then she walked over to the water pump and rinsed her mouth before she wiped a hand across her lips. Then she took a longer drink of water.

As Eleanor's cries drew her attention, her face reddened. Then she strode across the lawn toward me.

Heat warmed my neck and face at my ineptitude as a father. I almost prayed that God would open a fissure and let the ground swallow me whole.

"Need some help?" she asked as she neared.

"I could ask you the same."

Her cheeks turned red. "My stomach has been a little upset this morning. I'm fine."

I reached out and placed my hand on her forehead. Tingles spread through my arm at the touch. My breath shallowed as I remembered how much I had liked her in our school days. Somehow, I managed to clear my throat and speak.

"You don't feel warm."

She let out a slow breath. "I think my breakfast didn't agree with me. That's all."

Eleanor continued to wail.

"Won't take a bottle?" she asked.

I shook my head.

"Is she teething?"

"I… uh. How can I tell?" I inwardly cringed at the desperation in my voice.

Violet stepped closer until her side nearly pressed against mine. She placed a hand on the center of my back and fire radiated from her touch. Then she took her other hand and rubbed a finger on Eleanor's lips, then her gums.

When her hand dropped from my back, she stepped away. Her voice sounded breathy. "Yes, she's teething."

Then she moved to stand in front of me. "Try soaking a soft cloth with cool water. Then let her suck on it. When you get home, if you have any ice, that works even better."

I leaned down and looked through my bag.

"Like this?" I asked as I thrust the burping cloth at her.

She laughed. "Yes, that will do. Here. Let me take it to the pump."

As she walked away, I watched the sway of her hips. Heat settled on my face again as I scolded myself and averted my gaze. I was not some fifteen-year-old infatuated with the cutest girl in school. I was a father. A husband. Ugh. A widower.

When she came back, she took the damp part of the cloth and gently rubbed it on Eleanor's gums. "Like that."

I took over, and in a few more seconds, Eleanor rewarded me with quiet. I closed my eyes. "Thank God."

Violet laughed, a light sweet sound. "You're welcome."

When she started back toward the church, I wasn't ready for her to go. "How did you know what to do?"

"My son was a baby once."

"How old is he?"

"Will is about two and a half."

"Will. After your father?"

"Yes. You would have thought with five older brothers and one sort of adopted brother that the name would have been taken long before now. When it wasn't, I begged Forest that we honor Papa if we had a boy."

I shifted Eleanor to my other arm and resumed rubbing her gums with the soft cloth. "Forest Gamble, I presume?"

"Yes." Her face clouded as she looked toward the church building. "He passed in April."

Over two months ago. I remembered the early months. No sleep. No relief. Just grief and exhaustion. I wasn't even sure how often I made it to work in those early days.

"How long ago did your wife pass?"

My gaze snagged on those lovely blue eyes that made me want to take away her sorrow. The sympathy there nearly undid me. "Nine months."

"When Eleanor was born?"

I looked away and nodded.

"Does it get any better?" she asked.

My gaze returned to hers. I coughed to clear the emotion clogging my throat. "I'm not sure. I've just been trying to survive. Maybe now that I'm surrounded by family it will get better."

"I suppose having a newborn made it more difficult."

I snorted. "I'm not sure there is any benefit to quantifying grief, Violet. It's heart wrenching and painful and soul-crushing most days. I can only suppose it will get better one day because I see my mother with Jedediah. Their love gives me hope."

She laid a hand on my arm. "I'm sorry. I didn't mean to—"

"It's fine. I understand. Thank you for your help."

My terse words caused moisture to gather in the corners of her eyes. The guilt pressed in, but I ignored it. I had to put some distance between her and me because she came far too close to the most vulnerable spot in my heart. If I allowed anyone to see it, I would fall apart completely. Eleanor needed me too much. I had to keep it together for her sake.

Violet slowly backed away and headed into the church.

Another niggling of guilt broke through the thick crust over my heart. I prayed I had not wounded her too deeply with my words and that she would see them for what they were—protection for myself and Eleanor.

The next time I saw Violet, I should apologize to her. Especially since she would need every friend she had. I was positive her sickness was morning sickness and not because of some food she ate. She had that glow, the one that Rose had with each pregnancy. The one that preceded sickness. I swallowed hard. It was the glow that, in Rose's cases, preceded the shadow and days of darkness after another baby was lost. Four lost. One living.

A tear slid down my cheek and I wondered when I had become such an emotional man. I breathed a sigh of relief when the church doors opened and my family swarmed me. The loudness of them felt oddly comforting amid my silent heartache.

CHAPTER 6

VIOLET

I was in complete denial. I could not face the truth. The real reason my stomach was upset was obvious to me. I pushed the admission away from my conscience and commanded it to leave me alone, to let me live in denial for just a few more days. I needed to get through the pie competition at the upcoming Independence Day. My business needed that one milestone from me before I allowed the truth into my heart.

As I walked toward the water pump, I heard the screaming baby across the churchyard. Sounded like teething cries to me. Whoever the poor woman was, it must have been her first.

When I turned around and saw Zayne Harrison and his red-faced baby, I nearly tripped. Why hadn't his mother or sisters rescued him?

As I walked toward him, unexpected sympathy pressed on my heart. His eyes were wide, and frustration etched lines in his forehead. He was far too young to have lines in his forehead.

"Need some help?" I asked.

When he asked me the same, my face flushed. He had

seen me. So much for not embarrassing myself. I made up a lame excuse. Thankfully, his crying child distracted him before he discerned my lies.

Then I offered my help and a solution for Eleanor's teething. I was as relieved as he was when it worked.

Unfortunately, the next words out of my mouth clearly wounded Zayne. I had minimized his grief and compared it to my own. It was not my intention. I hated it when others did the same to me. Yet, I was so desperate to know if it got any easier; I said the worst things possible.

When he lashed out at me, I should have expected it. I deserved it. His situation was far worse than mine. He had an infant to raise amid his grief. No wonder he moved back to Prescott. It was the only way he was going to survive.

Me? I only lost my husband. A two-year-old was more manageable than a newborn. Not that his daughter was that young anymore.

Newborn. The word hit me as hard as a train speeding down the tracks. I stuffed the thought away. I still needed a few more days reprieve before dealing with the truth.

After Zayne's sharp words, I hurried back into the church. I squared my shoulders and pasted a smile on my face before I returned to my parent's pew. Once I sat down, Will curled against my side while the pastor continued with his sermon.

As soon as service was over, I gathered around my family outside. They made plans to meet on Wednesday at the Independence Day celebration. Sterling was going to be the pitcher for the Colter Cowboys baseball team instead of his father. So many things were changing.

My eyes searched the crowd until I found Zayne. His back faced me as he spoke with one of his sisters.

"Vi?"

"Pardon?" I asked when I missed Keri's question.

"Would you like to join us for supper today?"

"Yes, that would be nice," I said, as I really didn't want to go home and cook for just the two of us.

She smiled. "Good. James went to get the carriage. You and Will can ride with us."

Once supper finished, we excused the children to go play. Keri's nanny took Will up for a nap and I found myself a little jealous of my son. I could use a good nap.

After my third yawn, Keri said, "You should lie down in the guest room. You look weary."

"I don't want to be a terrible guest," I protested.

"You're family," James replied. "Family is always a terrible guest."

He chuckled at his own joke.

"Come." Keri tugged me up from the couch before she led me to the guest room. I didn't argue. Instead, I reclined onto the bed as she closed the door behind her.

Sometime later, I woke to a quiet and dark house. I rose and checked first in one bedroom then another. No one was upstairs. I rushed downstairs and breathed easier when I spotted the family gathered around the dining table for a game of cards.

Will sat on James's knee and read off the symbols on his cards.

"Heart."

James groaned. "You're not supposed to tell them my hand."

"Cub."

I laughed. "Club."

Will wriggled out of James's lap.

"Good grief, he's fast," James muttered. "How do you keep up with him?"

"I'm not old, like you. I still have good reflexes."

"She has a point," Keri said. "You are getting older."

James frowned. "Forty-one is far from old."

"But sweetheart, you are still young at heart," Keri added.

He harrumphed.

"I should go," I said. "Thank you for supper and the much needed rest."

Keri stood and joined me. "Are you sure we can't call a carriage for you?"

I shook my head. "It's not too far. We'll be fine."

"How does your stomach feel?" she asked.

My head snapped up. "Just fine. Thank you."

She studied my face for a minute. "It's just that you look like—"

"Thanks again," I interrupted her. I knew her well enough to know that she surmised my condition. I still was not ready to accept it.

She gave me a hug and led me to the door.

Will and I walked at a leisurely pace toward our house on the southeast side of town. As we walked, I noticed a man pushing a baby carriage. The closer I came, I recognized him.

"Zayne!" I called out as I picked up Will and jogged toward him.

"Oh, Violet, hello." He smiled.

"Out for a stroll?" I asked.

"Yes. Ella and I always take a walk on Sunday afternoon."

I smiled at his use of her nickname. It was the first I heard him call her that and it was beautiful.

"And you?"

"Just now headed home from James's house."

"And he didn't get you a carriage?" Zayne frowned.

"Oh, no. It's not that far. We are a short way up the street."

"Let me see you home," he said.

"Even though I upset you this morning?" The honest words flew from my mouth before I could retract them.

"I'm sorry about that. I'm not... It is hard to talk about Rose."

"I understand," I said, as he strode next to me.

"Can I ask you something?"

My stomach tightened for a moment. But I nodded anyway.

"Are you certain that your sickness this morning was from food?"

"Yes." I responded too quickly.

"It's just that..." He glanced over at me. My eyes begged him to stop.

"Never mind. It is not something that an unmarried man should talk about."

My throat tightened. He was far more observant than I credited him.

"This is us," I said as I stopped in front of my home.

"It's nice. Very welcoming."

My heart raced when he made no move to continue on. "I'm just a few houses up that street." He pointed to a large home on two lots. "That's it there."

"Oh, I did not know we were practically neighbors," I said as I set Will down. He opened the door and ran inside, leaving it hanging wide open behind him.

"Perhaps I'll see you on another walk soon," he said as he bid me farewell.

The idea sounded very appealing. I watched him as he walked up the street. When he turned around and waved at me, I smiled and waved back. How he knew I hadn't ducked into my house was beyond me. Then I entered my home and closed the door.

Zayne Harrison changed significantly from the schoolboy

who used to terrorize me with prank after prank. The new version of him was quite interesting. He was clearly a dedicated father. I had yet to see him without his daughter. And he apologized for his harsh words. The old Zayne never would have apologized for anything. Ever.

As I unpinned the hat from my head and set it aside, I sighed. I was going to take off Will's shoes, but he had already slipped them off and started playing with his blocks.

I took my hat into my room and returned it to its box. Then I went to the icebox and poured myself some iced tea. I sipped it as I continued to ponder the new man.

Those blue-gray eyes gave away nearly every thought on his mind. Of course, an uncontrolled crying infant could gnaw at the nerves of even the toughest of men.

Sometimes he seemed sad and desperate. At other times, hopeful.

Even though I took offense at his words about comparing grief, he was absolutely correct. Trying to quantify grief was useless. Not mine. Not his. It was just grief. Raw. Painful.

What had he called it? Oh, that's right. Soul-crushing. Only a man who experienced deep loss would know such a thing.

I smiled as I thought about the help I had provided. Relief was what his eyes communicated then. For once, I had done something kind for the man who had been unkind to me as a teenager.

Yet, even those old pranks seemed out of character for the man I met that morning. I doubted if he was unkind to a single soul.

I shook away the thoughts and joined Will on the floor to spend a few precious minutes playing with my son. Most nights, I was exhausted. Tonight, as I tried to ignore both versions of Zayne, I enjoyed the time with my son.

CHAPTER 7

VIOLET

When I woke up Monday morning, I could not deny the grim reality any longer. I was pregnant with my dead husband's child. I finally admitted the truth to myself as I heaved into a bucket just after my eyes opened.

Reality crashed in on me. I was too sick to open the pie shop by nine. I was too sick to bake the pies that I needed to bake for the holiday. Too sick to complete my masterpiece for the pie competition in two days.

I twisted my hair back into a loose bun at the base of my neck and secured it with a few pins just seconds before the next wave of nausea hit me.

"Mama!" Will cried from outside my door. His tentative cry quickly turned frantic when I didn't answer right away. "Mama!"

I stood and carried the bucket with me. Then I let him inside.

"Mama is feeling a little sick—"

I could not finish the sentence. Little baby Gamble took precedence over his or her older brother.

Will's eyes went wide.

"It's alright. In a few minutes, I'll be okay."

As I carried the bucket with me, Will followed me downstairs. Then I reached for the telephone and dialed Keri.

When her housekeeper answered, I whimpered, "It's me, Violet. Send Keri."

I placed the earpiece on the receiver before I lost it again.

Slowly, I shuffled to the sink to fill a glass with water. After I drank a few sips, I breathed deeply. When I rested my head in my hands, poor little Will cried. All my energy faded, and I let my son cry. My tears flowed as sorrow overwhelmed my soul. Oh, how I missed Forest and his tender care.

Ten minutes later, a knock sounded at my door.

"Violet?" Keri's voice sounded muffled by the door.

"Come in!" I called out, too weary to open it to greet her.

"Oh, my!" Keri rushed to my side.

She placed her arm on my forehead. "You aren't warm."

I shook my head. "Just with child."

She sighed heavily. "I'm so sorry, Vi. I thought you might be. Should I fix something for Will first?"

I nodded.

"Go lay down. Do you have another bucket?"

"Yes," I said as I grabbed it from the kitchen.

"Good. Leave that one here."

My feet felt heavy as I climbed the stairs. I set the other bucket near the side of the bed, then I laid down.

The sounds from downstairs echoed up the stairs. I could hear Keri on the telephone. I knew she wasn't much of a cook, since she grew up in a home with a hired cook and she employed one after marrying my brother.

"I see," she said. "So I boil the water and then add the oats?"

Silence.

"Uh, huh. Uh, huh."

Silence.

"At Violet's."

Silence.

"Oh, good. Yes. Just come in when you get here."

A few minutes later, another woman's voice drifted up to my room. It was Grady's wife, Justine. I let out a sigh of relief. She knew how to cook. She would care for Will.

I closed my eyes and fell asleep again.

When I went downstairs, Justine stood at the sink washing dishes.

"Where's Will?" I asked as my heart raced.

"Don't worry. Keri took him home with her. She thought she would save you the trip to drop him off later."

I blew out a breath.

"Do you want anything to eat?"

"No. I think I can get dressed and head to work."

"Are you sure? Katie already opened the shop for you."

"I need to go. I have lots of pies to bake for the holiday. And I still need to practice my competition pie at least one more time before I bake the final entry tomorrow."

Justine smiled. "You dress. I'll wait until you're ready, just in case."

"Thank you."

I glanced at the clock on the wall. Five after ten. I sighed as I climbed the stairs again. As I hurried through my morning routine, I tried to figure out how I was going to bake so many pies with such a late start.

When I returned downstairs, I felt a little queasy again. I pasted a smile on my face and thanked Justine. Then I reassured her I would be fine. We walked down the street for a few blocks until we split off.

The fresh air helped tremendously as I walked to the pie shop. It was ten-thirty by the time I arrived.

"Morning," Katie greeted me when she heard the back

door open. "How are you feeling?"

"Alright, I suppose."

"Keri mentioned your, um, condition."

I nodded slowly as my shoulders sagged.

"If you'd like, I will open the shop until you are ready to again."

"Thanks."

"Shall I watch the counter for the next inbound train? Or do you need help?"

"Watch the counter."

When she left, I sat on a stool for a minute. I wondered how I was going to manage the enormous task before me. Thankfully, I had purchased the supplies I needed several days ago, and my kitchen was fully stocked.

I reviewed my notes about how many pies I planned to make. The easiest was cherry, since I used my canned pie filling for that. So, that was where I started.

After an hour, all my symptoms completely vanished, and I moved about the kitchen in my usual efficient form.

"There's a man asking to see you," Katie said around twelve-thirty.

I frowned. "I'm really busy."

"I told him, but he insisted you need to take a break."

"Tell him I will be out soon."

I finished the lattice top of the last two cherry pies. Then I placed them in the oven and set the timer. I washed my hands and dried them on my apron as I walked to the front of the shop.

"Vi, have you eaten lunch yet?" James scolded me.

I looked away. "No."

"Come, sit and have lunch with me. It's Maria's famous chicken soup. She swears it will help you feel better."

I sighed heavily as I sank into a chair. "I guess that means

Keri told you what happened."

He smiled as he set a bowl of the still steaming soup in front of me.

"My wife and I have no secrets. When someone calls my house early in the morning, I find out what is going on. Eat up now."

As I sipped the soup, I felt better.

"Would you like me to hire someone to help you at home? Maybe for the short-term?"

I closed my eyes and took a deep breath. I let it out slowly and opened my eyes again.

"James, I'll be fine."

"You're pushing yourself too hard. Let me hire someone."

"You're sounding more like Papa than my big brother."

"Hey, big brothers watch out for their recently widowed, pregnant little sisters."

I glanced around. "Keep your voice down."

"If you want to live with us, that is also an option."

I finished the soup and frowned at him. "We've discussed this before. I'm not living off your charity. I have a home. And I will manage."

James leaned forward. "You look pale. Keri said she had never seen a woman so sick. What happens if you wake up tomorrow and feel the same, or even worse?"

I pushed the bowl toward him. Then I looked away. "I'll make due."

"But I'm offering you help so you do not need to suffer through it."

I stood, as I knew he would continue to press me until I caved in. "I have lots of work to do. Thank you for lunch."

He frowned. Then he stood and placed a kiss on my cheek, saying nothing more.

As I returned to the kitchen, he strode away. I resumed

baking and figured that was the end of it, until a knock sounded on the back door around half-past three.

"Vi!"

I sighed. "Just a minute, Mama!"

When I opened the door, my eyes burned instantly. There Mama stood with all my sisters-in-law: Ellie Mae, Jaclyn, Keri, Lilian, and Justine. The only one missing was Preston's wife, which made sense since they lived out of town.

Mama pulled me into a hug. "We've come to help."

"Who is watching the children?"

Ellie Mae laughed. "Most of mine are self-sufficient at this point. Sam can handle them."

"Of course mine are under the nanny's watchful eye," Keri said.

"Boone will somehow manage them with-out me for the evening," Jaclyn teased.

"You know how much Deacon loves his kids," Lilian said. "He seemed almost giddy when I asked him to head home early to watch them."

Justine laughed. "Big surprise here. Grady felt the same about ours."

We all laughed at that.

I dabbed at the moisture in the corner of my eyes. "Thank you for coming."

"Put us to work," Mama said.

In quick order, I started assigning tasks based on cooking skill. Mama helped with the crust. Since I used her original recipe, she knew it by heart and whipped up batch after batch of crust. Ellie Mae and Justine were excellent bakers, so I as-signed them the pie assembly. I knew they would meet my standards. Keri measured ingredients under Mama's watchful eye. Jaclyn gathered the ingredients for the filling and helped wash dishes as we went. I enlisted Lilian's help while I worked on my masterpiece, a chocolate cream pie.

"You are all sworn to secrecy about the ingredients in this pie," I warned them. Once they agreed, I started giving Lilian specific steps to help me.

"I need you to melt the chocolate over the double boiler. When it melts, put in one teaspoon of coffee grounds."

"Oh," Mama said. "I like that."

I smiled. "Stir vigorously until the chocolate melts. Let me know when it is almost ready so I can make sure I'm ready with the other ingredients."

She nodded.

As we worked, they talked, but I concentrated on my pie. I separated several egg whites and placed them in my mixing bowl. I added sugar and other ingredients. Then I whipped the mixture by hand until peaks formed. About when I was done, Lilian announced the chocolate was ready. I folded the mixture into the chocolate a little at a time. It turned out perfect. Then I scooped the mixture into a pie shell.

Next, I beat the ingredients for the meringue topping by hand after adding my two secret ingredients: vanilla and a touch of cinnamon. It was unconventional, but I loved to play with flavors. I was confident it would be a prize winner.

Then I placed it in the oven and took a seat on the stool.

"Cinnamon?" Mama asked. "I never considered that."

"In small amounts, it can enhance the vanilla and compliment the chocolate."

She smiled. "Do we get to taste test it?"

I grinned. "Absolutely. It's the least I can do to pay you all back for your help."

We worked for several more hours. By the time we finished, I had plenty of pies for the extra holiday traffic. The only baking I needed to do the next day was to make my official entry for the contest and extra chocolate cream pies to sell.

Justine brought the cooled chocolate cream pie over to the worktable and divided it so we would all get a bite. "I've been dying to try this."

They waited for me to take the first bite. When I did, I started coughing, well, fake coughing. "It's terrible. You'll hate it."

Then I smiled.

They each ate a bite. Then another.

"Vi, this is the best pie you've made yet," Mama said. "More than blue ribbon worthy."

"Yes," Keri agreed. "It's positively the most amazing pie I've ever eaten!"

The others complimented me as well. As I looked around the room, my heart warmed and eyes misted.

"Thank you, again, for all your help." I sniffed.

"We are all happy to pitch in," Keri said. "Just let us know. You don't have to do this all on your own."

"Yeah, we are here for you. I'm happy to come over and help you anytime," Jaclyn said. "Pearl can man the surveying office for me."

"Me, too," Justine said. "Keri has offered for me to take my kids to her place anytime, if Grady isn't available to watch them."

"We all want to support you," Lilian said. "So don't be afraid to ask us."

"You are part of this amazing family," Ellie Mae said. "We love you and would do anything for you."

"On that note," Mama said. "What do you say we get you home and feed you some supper?"

I smiled. "Sounds good to me."

I hugged each of them as they left.

Only Mama stayed behind. "I fixed up a cot in the empty

room for myself. I'll stay with you for a few days. Keri is going to keep Will for a few days, too."

"Oh, Mama!"

Tears streamed down my face as I tried to lock the door behind me. Mama took the key and locked it for me. Then we walked arm in arm back to my house.

As she set out bowls of stew on the table, which she must have put on the stove earlier in the day, she gave me that look.

"Violet, I don't know whether to offer you congratulations or empathy about your coming child."

I sniffed.

"But I want you to know that your entire family, me, Papa, your brothers and their wives, even your nieces and nephews, we are all here to help you in whatever way we can. When your time comes to deliver, I will be here for you. Keri, Justine, and Jaclyn are all a telephone call away. Ellie Mae and Lilian can help too. Even though they live on the ranch, they will come into town or watch Will at the ranch. Whatever you need."

"Thank you, Mama."

She stood and hugged me for a long moment.

"Just promise you will reach out when you need help."

"I promise."

CHAPTER 8

ZAYNE

"Mama!" I called for her as I hurried inside after my walk with Eleanor Monday evening.

"In here!" she called from the library.

"Is something wrong?" she asked when I appeared in the doorway.

"What? Oh, no."

Miss Harmony appeared. "Would you like me to put Miss Eleanor down for a nap, sir?"

When I handed her my daughter, my arms felt empty. I fought against the urge to see to the task myself. I moved home for the help, after all.

As I sat down, Mama asked what was on my mind.

After I nodded a greeting to Jedediah, I asked, "Do you have any connections with the organizers?"

"On the fourth?"

I nodded.

"Of course. So do you. One of them is your sister."

I leaned forward and frowned. "Which one?"

"Cora."

"Do you know when the pie competition will start?"

"Oh, yes. It'll be first thing in the morning. Around nine

like it always is."

My heart's pace sped up. "Do you think they could move it to eleven?"

Mama laughed. "Why are you so concerned about the pie contest?"

"Violet has entered the contest, right?"

"I can't divulge the participants. Wouldn't want to influence the judges." She jerked her head toward Jedediah, who looked up from his book and was now fully engaged in the conversation.

"I'm pretty sure she has morning sickness, and it's going to be hard—"

"Please tell me you did not discuss such a thing with her." Mama frowned at me. "It isn't polite."

I rubbed my hands on my knees. "What? No. We didn't. I just saw her at church." I sighed heavily. "Mama, I know the signs. Goodness knows I went through five pregnancies with Rose. I can spot—"

"Are you saying you think Violet Gamble is with child?"

"Yes. That is what I'm saying. And I think it diminishes her chance at winning an award if she has to deliver a fresh baked pie first thing in the morning. If they could move the contest back a few hours, it would help her."

Mama studied my face in silence for several minutes. Her lips parted a few times, but no sounds came out. At length she finally said, "I'm at a loss why this concerns you."

I sat up straight in my chair. "We're friends. I'm just trying to help a friend. That's all."

Mama narrowed her eyes. I felt as if her gaze bore through to the depths of my soul, just like when I lied to her as a teen.

"I'll see what I can do."

I stood and placed a kiss on her cheek. "Thank you."

On Wednesday, I took my time getting ready for the celebration. There was no need for me to rush. I only wanted to see the pie competition. Mama had convinced Cora, who convinced the committee to move it closer to lunchtime. It was a brilliant argument, and I wished I had thought of it when I enlisted Mama's help.

"Mr. Harrison," Harmony got my attention as I placed Eleanor in her carriage. "Whenever you want a break or if you want me to bring her home for a nap, you just let me know. I'll make sure I'm close by. But not hovering."

"Thank you, Harmony. I appreciate it."

Even though I wasn't trying to hurry, I was still the first one out. I strolled with the carriage leisurely toward Violet's home before I even realized it.

I saw her head over the fence line. As I drew near, I heard her throwing up. My heart ached for her, as I knew from the experience with Rose that it could last for days or weeks. It drained a woman.

I continued on toward the location of the festivities. I smiled, feeling good that I had eased her burden.

After the thought hit my heart, I wondered when that mattered to me. I reminded myself that we were friends. We went to school together. I had known her most of my life. Well, all but the last ten years.

Still, I knew grief, and I knew Violet needed all the help she could get. Especially if I was right about her condition. It could be lonely to care for a newborn on your own.

And she was a woman alone. Trying to figure out how to provide for her toddler son and herself. There would be questions once her condition became known. People would judge her and count the months and try to guess if Mrs. Violet Gamble carried her late husband's child or one from another man. It was harsh. Busybodies came up with lies to enliven their own dull lives without regard for those they hurt.

So, if my interference helped give Violet a fighting chance at winning that pie contest, then I would not feel ashamed in the slightest.

Eleanor cooed from the security of her carriage.

"Well said!" I encouraged her as if she read my thoughts of the past several minutes.

When I arrived at the fair, I found the tables that Loren reserved as our home base for the day. A few of my sisters had already set out baskets with plates and silverware and snacks for their little ones. It would be wonderful to see the whole family. Only Rose and Papa were missing.

Wilma and Alice arrived at the same time with their families. Wilma smiled down at Eleanor. "She's so adorable. Is she feeling any better since Sunday?"

"Yes, now that I know how to help her, she is doing just fine."

She smiled warmly. "I heard what you did for Violet. I think it is very sweet."

I rolled my eyes. "How did you find out?"

"Well, Cora told Alice and Alice told Beulah, and you know Beulah can't keep a secret."

I sighed. "Does the whole town know?"

"Oh, no. But every Harrison does."

She squeezed my shoulder. "We always thought you'd marry her. The way you carried on in school. Plain as day that you loved her back then."

My sister Pearl called to her, and she hurried away as my heart lodged in my throat.

"Can I see her, Uncle Zayne?" Victoria's oldest girl asked.

"Certainly, Georgiana."

"Hello, Eleanor," she said as she reached into the carriage and lifted her into her arms. "I can hardly wait until I have one of my own."

"Don't you think you should find yourself a husband first?"

Her cheeks turned red, and she smiled. "Wedding bells are in my near future."

"Congratulations!" Before I asked who the lucky young man was, Loren's wife welcomed me home and asked to see Eleanor.

They passed Eleanor from aunt to aunt to cousin to aunt for the next twenty minutes. At last, I rescued my little girl saying she needed a nap.

"The pie competition winners are about to be announced," Cora told me.

I saw Harmony nearby, and she came over to watch Eleanor.

Then I joined my sister near the podium for the announcement of the winners. Violet stood nearby. She looked exhausted and a little pale. My stomach tightened. I worried she was pushing herself too much. She needed someone to take care of her, instead of trying to manage a business, a son, and a baby on the way by herself.

She offered me a smile when I caught her gaze. My heart flipped upside down.

Mayor Ward invited Violet and two other women to the stage, along with Cora. Cora held ribbons for first, second, and third place. Mayor Ward announced the third place winner.

"For her classic cherry pie, third place goes to..." He paused as the crowd silenced. "Miss Martha Simpson!"

The crowd cheered as Cora pinned the ribbon to Miss Simpson's dress. Violet clasped the hand of the woman next to her.

"Second place goes to the perfectly tart berry pie made by..." Again a pause. "Mrs. Henrietta White!"

Another cheer went up as Cora pinned her ribbon on.

Violet's eyes went wide. She realized, as I did, that she was the first prize winner.

"For her innovative and scrumptious chocolate cream pie, the first-place winner is Mrs. Violet Gamble!"

The crowd roared. Mayor Ward took the ribbon from Cora, clearly going off the script, judging by my sister's momentary frown. Then he fumbled awkwardly to pin the ribbon on Violet's dress. Her smile disappeared as his hand lingered on her shoulder.

I frowned and wanted to walk up to the mayor and haul him off the stage for his deplorable behavior.

Instead, I ran to the edge of the platform. Violet smiled at me and I reached up to help her off the stage. Instead of helping her down the stairs, I took her into my arms and twirled her around in a circle before I set her feet on the ground.

"Zayne!" She rewarded me with a breathy laugh and a broad smile.

"Congratulations, Violet." My voice revealed the depth of my feelings—feelings that I should deny.

As the noise of the crowd faded, my hands remained on her waist. I swallowed away the dryness in my mouth as I studied her brilliant blue eyes. They sparkled in the light, matching the vibrant glow of her skin. I wanted to pull her closer and kiss her.

The thought terrified me, and I immediately released my hold as I chastised myself for so quickly forgetting my beloved Rose. I mumbled an apology as I rubbed the back of my neck. Then I backed up a few paces before I turned on my heels and retreated to the safety of my family's picnic tables.

Fool. Stupid. Fool.

Surely my inappropriate and very public behavior mortified her. She was a widow. Her husband passed three short months ago. She was far from over mourning his loss.

I clenched my fist at my side as I slid onto the bench at the table closest to Eleanor's carriage.

It must have been Wilma's comment about loving Violet that caused my judgment to flee from me faster than a runaway wagon. I should expect Violet to never speak to me again, even if I showed up at her pie shop.

I caught Mama's eye, and she smiled. My mama downright grinned and gave me a knowing look. I shook my head. Perhaps all the Harrisons had gone mad that day.

CHAPTER 9

VIOLET

As I carried my chocolate cream pie to the pie table the morning of the fourth of July, I breathed a sigh of relief. What a godsend that they moved the competition to eleven that year. I was unsure if I would have been able to deliver my entry. The morning sickness hit me hard earlier in the day, but by ten o'clock it subsided.

My brothers helped me carry several pies from the shop to a table at the festivities. Whether my pie won a prize, folks would stand in line to buy some. If it won, I could charge thirty-five cents for a slice, and I would definitely sell out.

I really hoped I placed. I believed my creation would stand out among the other pies. One could not tell if my pie was special by looking at it. But once the judges bit into it, I was certain they would love it.

I paced nervously back and forth by my pie table as I waited for the results. At long last, the committee organizer and Mayor Ward stood on the podium. They motioned for me and two other women to join them.

Mayor Andrew Ward, the man who stood me up at my wedding, was the announcer. I wished it was anyone else. Unfortunately, he specifically asked the committee for the privilege to announce the winners of the pie contest.

I sighed as I stepped onto the podium. I noticed Zayne watching me and I smiled. He looked rather fetching despite his casual white cotton shirt and tan trousers with suspenders. He smiled at me, and my pulse quickened.

When they announced third place, my hands grew sweaty. Then they announced second place. Not me. Wait. That meant.

"First place, Violet Gamble!"

I grinned as I stepped forward. Then my smile faded as Andrew grabbed the ribbon and insisted on pinning it on my dress. His hand lingered uncomfortably long on my shoulder as he whispered in my ear.

"You look stunning today."

Clearly, he had forgotten about our history and the fact that I abhorred him. And that he had married Catherine.

"Perhaps you wouldn't mind bringing one of those pies to my home tomorrow?"

I nodded numbly. Then I walked to the edge of the platform.

Zayne hurried to help me down. When he placed his hands on my waist, my breath left in a rush. Then he pulled me into his arms and twirled me around. My pulse hurled to a speed I never felt before.

"Zayne!" I laughed as he set me down. My hands remained on his shoulders for one heartbeat. Then two.

"Congratulations." His voice was husky as I stared into his blue-gray eyes.

I licked my lips, as I could not bring myself to move away from the intensity of his gaze.

Suddenly, he dropped his hold.

"I'm sorry. So sorry."

He retreated out of my sight after backing away.

"He's the one that convinced the committee to move the time," his sister Cora whispered to me in passing.

I raised an eyebrow as I wondered if I heard her correctly. She was gone before I could ask questions.

"Vi!" Boone hollered. "How much you selling these for?"

I hurried over to my pie table. "Thirty-five cents a slice," I answered as I divided the pies into slices. I grabbed one piece in my hand before I told my family I would be right back.

Then I strode toward the picnic tables. It was easy to spot the Harrison clan. My, how their family had grown. I quickly scanned the tables and found Zayne seated at the edge of a table. Of course, Eleanor was in her carriage right next to him.

I cleared my throat to get his attention. When he looked up, he failed to mask the shock on his face. As I set the piece of pie in front of him, he dug in his pockets for change. I placed a hand on his arm and he froze.

Then I leaned forward and whispered, "It's on me. It is the least I can do for you. Thank you for what you did for me."

He frowned.

"Cora told me."

Recognition dawned on his face.

"I think you will like it," I said as I stepped back. "I heard the lady that baked it won first prize."

I watched as he took the first bite. He closed his eyes and savored it. When he opened his eyes, he complimented me, and I flashed him a smile before I ran off to sell more pies.

As I let out a slow breath, I felt incredibly humbled. He somehow convinced Cora to push the pie competition back. For me. Zayne Harrison.

I shook my head. The same Zayne Harrison who persuaded me as a schoolgirl to try some magical cream that would make my face shine. It was magical, alright. My cheeks were rosy and red for two days. I never figured out what it was.

Yeah, that Zayne Harrison moved a mountain to make my morning easier.

"What's got you grinning like a fool?" Boone teased me as he collected some change from a patron.

Warmth spread across my face. "I won first place, if you recall."

"Yeah, that ain't it."

———

The next few days felt like a whirlwind. Thankfully, my morning sickness was manageable. The shop was busier than normal. We sold out of the pies my family helped me bake. I spent the better part of two days baking pie after pie. On the day after the holiday, Mama helped me. Then Justine came by in the afternoon. Keri even helped man the front counter on Friday so Katie could help me in the kitchen.

I made it through those busy days with little energy left in the evenings. Keri sent supper home with me each day when I picked up Will. It was a tremendous relief to have food ready to eat when we arrived home.

On Friday afternoon, despite my exhaustion, I sat in the rocker on my front porch, while Will played with his blocks. I was watching him and failed to notice someone approach.

"Good evening."

My head jerked up. When I saw who it was, I beamed. "Good evening, Zayne."

"Would you care for a stroll?"

My breath left me. I nodded as I pulled the door closed.

When I reached down to pick up Will, he interjected, "Let me carry him and you can push the carriage?"

"I'm surprised you would trust me with Eleanor."

He laughed. "So, you've noticed I tend not to let her out of my sight."

I snorted. "Or your arms."

He sighed heavily. "I'm just so used to being the only one to care for her."

"You know how mothers feel."

He chuckled. Then his joviality disappeared. "When I return to work on Monday, I don't know what to do."

"Oh? Surely your mother or someone in the house will watch her."

"It's not someone else watching her that concerns me. It's leaving her."

I made funny faces at Eleanor as we walked. Then I said, "It gets easier after a while. It is difficult the first few times."

"How are things at the shop?" He moved closer to me and rested a hand on the carriage handle near mine but not touching it.

"Bird!" Will startled Zayne before he giggled.

"Does he shout out often?"

"Oh, yes. And he thinks every word is the funniest thing."

We walked for a few feet in silence.

Zayne cleared his throat. "What did Mayor Ward say to you on the podium that made you frown?"

I let out a long breath. "Truthfully?"

"Yes, I want to know."

"He told me I looked stunning."

Zayne stopped and faced me as he frowned. "He's married."

"Oh, don't I know it."

I nudged the baby carriage forward, and he fell into step beside me again.

"We have history. A history which he seems to forget."

I rubbed my hand along the length of the carriage handle.

"When I was nineteen, he proposed to me. We were supposed to get married." I sniffed. "Then he ran off with Catherine Parker the night before our wedding day."

"Seems like that would be kinda hard to forget," he said wryly.

"For me or for him?"

"For everyone."

I let out a long breath. "You would think. When his wife isn't around, he makes suggestive comments."

Zayne straightened next to me. "That's wrong."

"That's Andrew. He always wants what he does not have. Possibly doesn't want what he has."

He cleared his throat. "Do you still have feelings for him?"

I laughed. "Heavens no. When a man stands up a woman for a wedding, he is dead to her."

I quickly changed the topic, as I wanted to stop thinking about those painful memories.

"Anyway, how are you settling in, besides being nervous about leaving Eleanor?"

"Well enough, I suppose. It's rather unusual being back home after all this time. The house is nearly the same. The people… Papa is gone and Jedediah is nice, but he's not Papa."

Eleanor cooed, then settled back to sleep.

"I'm a grown man living with his mother and her new husband. So it takes some adjusting."

"But I'm sure you are glad for the help."

"I am. I feel like I can finally breathe for the first time in a year."

I yawned, and Zayne caught me.

"You must be worn out. Let's get you back home."

"Tree!" Will giggled.

"I guess he has only one volume, too."

I snorted. "Reminds me a bit of my brother Boone."

Zayne laughed. "I can see it."

When we arrived back at my house, he set Will down. Will ran inside, but I stood still. Despite my weariness, I wasn't ready for Zayne to leave. His eyes studied mine for several seconds. Then he leaned forward and kissed my cheek.

"I best get Eleanor down for the night," he said. "See you around."

"Good night."

I stood there and watched him push the carriage up the hill toward his house. When he stopped in front of it, he turned and waved.

I sighed and waved back.

CHAPTER 10

ZAYNE

The walk with Violet was rather nice. She was easy to talk to. Her son was adorable. Birds. Trees. I shook my head.

As I pushed Eleanor's stroller up the hill, I could not resist the urge to look back toward Violet's house. It surprised me when I saw her still standing on her porch. I smiled and waved to her, though I doubted she could see my smile from that distance. When she waved back, I treasured it.

I carefully lifted the carriage onto the porch and pushed it inside. Before I could reach in and take Eleanor into my arms, Harmony appeared.

"There you are. Should I take her up?"

I hesitated. Then I chastised myself. If I never accepted help, then it was foolish of me to have moved home. I nodded, and Harmony wrapped Eleanor in her fleshy arms and carried her away.

"It's good to see you smile when you came in." Mama got my attention from her chair near the cold fireplace. "It was a pleasant walk, then?"

I smiled. "Yes. I ran into Violet Gamble. She and her son joined us on our walk."

Mama's eyes lit up. "Oh?"

I debated whether to say more.

She patted the side table next to her. "Come sit with me for a while."

"Where's Jedediah?"

"In the library. He wanted to pen some letters to his children."

I sat in the chair on the other side of the table.

"So, you start work on Monday?" she asked, even though we had discussed it several times.

"Yes."

"How is Violet? I heard her pie shop was very busy for the rest of the week."

"She's remarkably well, considering she's lost so much." I gazed at the empty fireplace. Had it been cooler, I would have started a fire for the ambience.

"Do you think you will visit with her again soon?"

I glanced over at Mama. She was fishing.

"I'm not sure. Her house is at the bottom of the hill. It wouldn't surprise me to run into her again."

"Perhaps you should leave Eleanor here sometime tomorrow and visit her at the pie shop. Just not when the train arrives."

I rubbed a hand on my chin. It was a delightful idea. If she wasn't too busy, I'd like to visit with her.

"You don't think it's too soon after her husband's passing to be seen with me?"

Mama smiled. "If she's open to being seen with you for a walk, I doubt very much she's concerned about what others think."

I considered her words. "Perhaps I will see if she has any of that chocolate cream pie. It was rather delicious."

"I wouldn't know. She sold out at the fair before I purchased a piece."

I sighed. "Can I ask you something?"

"Of course."

"When Jedediah first started courting you, did you ever feel guilty? Like you were being unfaithful?"

Mama's smile faded. She looked out the window for a moment.

"Yes. Falling in love a second time, after such a loss, is a strange and complicated thing. It is like falling in love for the first time. In other ways, it feels strange. My mind knows there is nothing wrong with falling in love as a widow. Yet, sometimes my heart felt like I was betraying Joshua."

"I still think about Rose a lot, Mama. I loved her..." I coughed away the tears that threatened. "Still do. It's hard to believe she is really gone forever."

Mama reached over and squeezed my hand.

"When I first saw Violet, she captivated me again. It's been ten years since we were in school together. Yet, those feelings..."

"You never stopped loving her. You only for-got about her when you went to the University of Arizona."

"I thought about her often those first few months at university. Many times, I wondered if I should write to her. I wasn't brave enough to ask if I could before I left."

I rubbed my hand on the arm of the chair.

"Then I met Rose. Rose was there. She was real. Tangible. And totally smitten with me. I forgot all about Violet and fell in love with Rose."

Mama sat in silence so I continued, "I always thought that maybe I never really loved Violet. When I was eighteen, I believed I did. But I figured if I forgot about her so easily, per-haps I never did."

Mama took a breath and let it out slowly. "Zayne, I think you loved her as much as a teenager knows and understands love. But you and she had different lives to live."

I frowned. "I know little of her story. But what I know, it seems like she has faced more heartache than most people her age. More than even I've faced."

I turned my head to meet my mother's gaze. "Is it strange to want to pick up my friendship with her after all this time?"

"Not at all. It seems like you already have."

"Is that why you suggested I visit her tomorrow?"

Mama laughed. "Of course. I watched how you looked at her. I saw you pick her up and twirl her around. That's a little more than just friendship, don't you think?"

"I suppose so."

"Just spend time with her. Get reacquainted with her. See if she develops similar feelings for you. But don't overthink it. The heart doesn't always follow a logical pattern."

I laughed. "No, it does not."

———

The next afternoon, I headed over to the train station. I left Eleanor with Mama and Harmony.

When I arrived, the train station was fairly quiet. I made my way to Violet's pie counter. I didn't see anyone around, so I rang the bell and waited patiently as I studied the delicious-looking pies.

"Can I help you?" Katie said as she stepped behind the counter.

"Is Violet around?" I asked.

"She's in the kitchen just finishing up a batch of pies. Should I tell her you're here?"

"Yes. If you have a piece of chocolate cream pie, I will take it."

"Of course."

Once I paid her for the pie, she handed me the plate and went into the kitchen. As I sat down, Katie told me Violet would be out shortly. I used the fork to cut off a bite of the pie. Then I placed it in my mouth and savored it. The texture was creamy. The flavor was delightful, just like the woman who created it.

"Zayne, how can I help you?" Violet said as she stood across from me.

"You can't." I winked at her.

She raised an eyebrow. "Please tell me this isn't one of your pranks."

I frowned but quickly wiped it away. "No. I came by to see you. Well, and for a slice of pie."

Her cheeks tinged with rosy circles. "Me?"

I nodded. "Do you have time to visit with me?" I motioned the chair across from me.

She wrung her hands together. "I…"

"The next train doesn't arrive for several hours." I stood and held out the chair for her.

"I suppose I could." She glanced at the kitchen.

I sat down and clasped her hand. "Katie can pull the pies from the oven, can't she?"

"Um. Yes."

I flashed one of my more charming smiles. "Good. Stop worrying and enjoy a break."

She frowned as I lifted a bite of pie to my mouth. I returned the fork to the plate without eating it.

"Have I offended you?"

I studied her face. She looked away. Then she opened her mouth. Then closed it. I waited.

"Yes. Well, no. Not recently."

"But at some point, I have offended you."

I thought through all our interactions since I returned to

Prescott and came up empty.

"Did I miss greeting you somewhere?"

She shook her head. "No."

"Did I slight you?"

"No."

"You're going to have to give me something, Vi."

She cleared her throat. Katie brought us both coffee and set a piece of pie in front of Violet. She smiled and waited for Katie to leave.

"It's just that… When we were in school, you were so cruel to me."

I choked on the piece of pie in my mouth. "I was?"

She frowned and crossed her arms. "You don't remember putting frogs in my lunch pail? Or a snake in my coat? Or pulling my braids at nearly every recess?"

I remembered doing those things. But I did not know it bothered her.

"You always smiled after every prank," I said.

She sighed in disgust. "Because I didn't want you to know how hurt I felt. I decided I would smile and not let you see how much it bothered me. I figured if you thought it didn't bother me, then you would stop."

I laughed and immediately knew that was the wrong response. "I kept doing those things *because* you smiled at me. You were the prettiest girl in the entire school, and you only paid attention to me when I teased you."

She harrumphed. "You mean to tell me you kept doing those things because I kept smiling at you?"

I took another bite of pie, and the creamy deliciousness momentarily distracted me. "This is so good. You really are an amazing baker."

Violet snorted and uncrossed her arms. She sipped her coffee. "You should have tried that tactic back then."

I raised an eyebrow.

"Complimenting me."

"Are you going to eat that?" I asked about the piece of cherry pie in front of her. She pushed it across the table to me.

"I'll pay you for it."

"It's unnecessary."

I took a bite of the cherry pie. So tart. That fluffy crust. If I kept spending time with her, my waistline was going to expand.

"This is the best cherry pie I've ever eaten."

"Better than your mama's?"

I laughed. "My mother is a terrible cook. Or she used to be. I can't recall her ever trying to make a pie."

Violet's eyes rounded. "You never ate pie?"

"I didn't say that. Our cook made good pies. But none of them hold a candle to yours."

At last, a smile from Violet Gamble. I tucked that image away for later. Seemed I still went to great lengths to be rewarded with her smile.

"About our school days. I honestly believed you did not mind any of those pranks. You were a good sport to put up with my pranks and come out smiling. I'm sorry I hurt you."

She reached across and squeezed my hand. "Thank you."

As she sipped the coffee, she glanced away. Her shoulders sagged.

"I suppose I should thank you for those pranks. When I think back on them, they really helped me become resilient. They prepared me for the humiliation of Andrew's rejection and Cooper's disappearance."

I ate the last bite of cherry pie before I took a swig of my coffee. "I thought Gamble's name was Forest."

Her gaze locked on mine. "It was."

"Who was Cooper?" I wondered how many suitors she

had over the years.

"He was my second love. I met him in 1900." She sighed. "He was charming and funny."

"When I moved into town, I stayed at the boardinghouse and worked in the cafeteria at the railroad offices. Shocking as it sounds, I baked pies."

"Indeed. Seems unlikely you would do such a thing."

She laughed.

"Anyway, Cooper worked in the traffic department. He often came to lunch later than most employees because his schedule revolved around the train timetables. So, I was usually cleaning up. He used to come into the kitchen and flirt with me while I washed dishes."

Her eyes dimmed. "We fell in love, and he proposed. Then he disappeared."

I fought against the urge to hunt the idiot down, if for no other reason to force him to apologize.

"The great fire that summer swept through the business district a few weeks before our wedding. No one saw him after that night. His bank account was empty. His horse was gone. And so was he."

"What happened?"

"To this day, I still don't know. His untimely departure created a lot of issues for me besides a broken heart. The house that he bought was in his name only. I had to beg and plead with the territory's attorney to allow me access to retrieve the things I had already moved in. After giving up my room at the boardinghouse, I had to move out. I ended up moving in with James and Keri."

My heart ached for her. My losses seemed insignificant compared to hers.

"Anyway, I should thank you. All those years of pranks at school. Of feeling humiliated. That pales compared to being stood up twice just shy of my wedding day."

After I reached over and took her hands in mine, I rubbed my thumb over her knuckles. "I'm so sorry."

She pulled away from my touch and waved her hand in the air. "Don't be. You aren't the one that left me at the altar, so to speak."

"No. But I can imagine how incredibly painful that was."

"And now that Forest—" her voice cracked, "is gone, I can't imagine ever marrying again."

Her words cut to the center of my heart. I hoped they were not true, and that it was just her grief speaking. I realized then how much I wanted them not to be true.

"I'm sorry," she said as her tears fell. She stood and hurried back to her kitchen.

I let her go. There would be other opportunities to show her she could trust me.

CHAPTER II

VIOLET

Monday morning dawned. I overslept and bolted upright in my bed. I dressed in my black mourning gown and entered Will's room to wake him. He groaned and rolled over. I nudged him again.

"No!"

I sighed and scooped my belligerent son from his bed. He squirmed and fussed while I tried to dress him.

"Please, Will, settle down. We're late." I knew it was silly to reason with my almost three-year-old.

It was after ten by the time I had him dressed. I skipped making him breakfast. I hoped Keri wouldn't mind feeding him.

As we walked toward James's house, Will kept going limp like he wanted to sit on the ground. I finally picked him up, and he started pulling my hair. When I shifted him to the other hip, he pulled my hair on that side. A few houses away from James's, Will pushed away from me. My grip on him loosened, and he fell to the ground, screaming. I kneeled, dusted him off, and checked for any injuries. Thankfully, I found none. I held his hand the rest of the way.

When Keri opened the door, she gasped.

"Is it that bad?" I asked.

"Come in. There's a mirror in the washroom that you can use to fix your hair."

"Thank you. I'm sorry, I didn't have time to feed him."

"I can see he's been a handful already," she said sympathetically as I headed down the hall.

I stood in front of the mirror. Goodness, my hair! I quickly unpinned the mess and finger combed it. Then I braided it before wrapping it around my head. After pinning it back in place, I hurried out the door.

As I walked toward work, I ran into none other than Andrew Ward. My day was only getting worse.

"Violet. It disappointed me you never stopped by last week with that pie."

"I was quite busy keeping up with the influx of customers at the store."

He slowed his pace to match mine. I glanced around, hoping no one saw us together. I didn't want to be seen walking alone with the mayor.

"Catherine was away visiting her sister. I was hoping to be alone with you."

My skin crawled at the slick way he spoke to me. "It would have been rather inappropriate."

He touched my arm and pulled me into the closest alley.

"I still love you, Violet. I always have."

I placed my hands on my hips. "You certainly failed to show it when you left me at the altar."

He glanced away. "That was a mistake."

After he rested one hand on my waist, he pulled me tight. I flattened my palms on his chest and shoved hard, but he didn't loosen his grip.

"I shouldn't have done that."

"Let me go."

"I know you still have feelings for me."

I slapped him hard across the face. Then I brought my foot down on his arch. He released me and groaned. I ran out of the alley and down the street as tears burned my eyes. What a horrible, horrible man.

When I arrived at the pie shop, my stomach turned over. I threw up before I entered the building, though I wasn't certain if it was from my baby or from nerves.

"Violet? Is that you?" Katie called from the front counter.

"Yes."

The telephone rang, and I listened as Katie answered it. "I see. We will see to it today."

She walked back to the kitchen as I finished drinking some water.

"That was the mayor's secretary."

When I set the glass down hard on the counter, Katie raised an eyebrow while she studied me for a few seconds.

"What did the mayor's office want?" I asked, even though I was certain I knew.

"The mayor wants to know when you are going to bring the chocolate cream pie that you promised."

I sighed heavily. "And you told his secretary today?"

"Yes, we have a few in stock."

"I'll see to it after I start a few pies in the oven."

Katie helped me prepare several pies. We didn't speak. My thoughts were too tumultuous to share while I worked. My life was entirely upside down. My husband was gone. I carried his unborn child. Our son expressed his grief through stubbornness. And now Andrew Ward pursued me despite his marital status.

The thought of Andrew Ward made my stomach churn. I knew he would pester me until I brought him a pie. I ought to see to it today, but the thought of going to his house made me ill whether Catherine was home. If she was gone, I feared what he would do to me. If she was home, I knew she would demean me. It was an impossible situation.

After thirty minutes, I put the fresh strawberry pies in the oven. The aroma would soon fill the train station and draw weary travelers to my shop. Nothing welcomed a person like the smell of fresh baked pie.

At last, I opened the pie safe and grabbed one of the chocolate cream pies. I squared my shoulders and walked out of the shop. As soon as the sun hit my face, nausea overwhelmed me. I stumbled and the perfect pie flew out of my hands. Then I threw up all over the destroyed pie.

Slowly, I sank to my knees and buried my face in my hands. All the anxiety and grief of the past few months pushed into my heart. Sorrow. Grief. Loneliness.

Oh, how I missed Forest. He would comfort me. If I told him about Andrew, he would have put the vile man in his place. He would have delivered the pie in my stead. He would have protected me.

Instead, he was gone. It left me to face Andrew alone. No one to help me. No one to keep me safe.

"Are you alright?"

I turned my gaze up to the man who stood over me. His gentle voice instantly warmed my heart. The sun cast a glow around him. He looked like an angel, sent there to rescue me in my time of need.

As he kneeled beside me, I poured out my heart to him, hoping that just maybe I could trust him with it.

CHAPTER 12

ZAYNE

After breakfast Monday morning, I walked the length of the parlor with Eleanor in my arms.

"I'm going to miss you, baby girl," I whispered to her.

Mama entered the room. "You're going to be late."

When Mama held out her hands, I cuddled Eleanor closer. I wanted to hold her longer.

"Here," Mama whispered. "Give me Eleanor."

She practically had to pull my girl out of my arms.

"Go. She'll be fine with us. I promise."

Then I took one step toward the door. And another. As I opened the door, I glanced over my shoulder.

"Say bye-bye to your Papa."

As Eleanor cooed, my heart tugged and I coughed. I straightened my back. Then I walked out the door.

Once outside, I set a brisk pace to the office. When I arrived, the office was a flurry of activity. We had both inbound and outbound freight at the same time. I sighed. There would be no peaceful transition back to work.

Smalley loaded the outbound freight headed east by wagon. Several other employees unloaded the inbound freight into the warehouse.

"Morning, Uncle Zayne."

"Morning, Albert," I greeted Victoria's oldest son. He was only four years younger than me.

"I go by Al these days. When the chaos settles, I'll bring you up to speed on what's going on."

"How can I help?"

He told me the morning train was due in twenty minutes and that he needed someone to receive the freight from the train and bring it over to the warehouse.

"Normally, I would do it, but this needs my attention."

"No problem."

"You can take Oscar and Jake with you." He quickly introduced me to the two men.

I looked over the paperwork. We would need two wagons, so we hitched up the teams and started toward the freight dock at the train depot.

I sighed. I wondered if it was wrong for me to take over the office. Martin had been grooming Al for the position. He was doing a fine job as the interim manager in the few months since Martin had moved down to Tucson. It didn't seem fair to me to come in and take over. Especially not since my life was such a mess.

The train whistle blew and pulled me out of my pensive thoughts. When it arrived, I marked off each crate as Oscar and Jake loaded them into the wagon. There was one missing crate, so I went to see if the freight manager knew where it was.

If it turned up, he would call the office. I held back a sigh. Missing freight was to be expected from time to time. It was never resolved quickly. If they didn't find it in that shipment, we would have to file a claim. In return, our customer would file a claim against us.

As I walked past the station building, the pie shop's back

door opened. I glanced at my pocket watch, then at the door. I headed toward it to see what was happening.

When Violet exited with a pie in her hands, she doubled over. The pie fell to the ground, splattering all over the sidewalk right before she threw up. As she sank to her knees, I hurried over to her.

"Are you alright?"

She turned red-rimmed eyes to face me. Then she sniffed loudly as she dabbed her mouth with the corner of her apron.

"No." Her voice squeaked.

My heart broke. I kneeled beside her and rubbed a hand on her back.

"I'm all alone. My husband is gone. My son is a handful. I'm carrying Forest's unborn child, which is making me sick for hours every morning."

Her voice cracked. "And now I've ruined the mayor's pie!"

I stiffened at the mention of Mayor Ward.

Her cries turned to sobs as I wrapped my arm around her shoulders. Then I helped her to her feet.

"Come inside," I suggested. She would be even more embarrassed if she noticed the growing number of witnesses gawking across the way.

After I led her to a stool, I retrieved the pie tin for the dam-aged pie. Then I entered her kitchen and closed the door behind me. I found a glass and filled it with some water. Then I handed it to her.

"I'm so sorry," she managed between sobs. "My life. Is a. Mess."

I nodded.

She frowned as her ire rose. "Are you agreeing with me?"

Guess it was the wrong thing to do. *She's not Rose.*

Perhaps humor would help. "I mean, look at what a mess it is. You run a successful pie shop. At the fair, you won the first prize. And you sold out of your inventory late last week."

She snorted.

I smiled. "Your dashing friend even stopped by at just the right time. How much worse could it get?"

I winked at her, and she finally rewarded me with one of her thrilling smiles.

After she straightened her shoulders, she sipped water for a few minutes. I leaned against the counter near her. Then I brushed a wayward strand of her hair back from her face.

"I suppose you're mostly right."

I quirked an eyebrow.

"About everything except the dashing friend. A little humility goes a long way, Zayne."

I laughed. "I don't think anyone has ever accused me of being humble."

She snorted.

"In all seriousness, Violet, you are doing great. Your family will do whatever they can to help you. I know it seems like a lot to deal with right now." I cleared my throat. "Especially coming to terms with the reality of carrying a child alone."

She looked down at her hands. I leaned into her line of sight until she looked at me, then I backed away.

"But you aren't alone. You have family in town. I'm right up the street." I snorted. "From both your work and your home. Anything you need, ask."

"I need a husband."

The words slammed into my heart. I straightened as I held my breath.

"My husband."

I let out my breath slowly and willed my heart to stop racing. "You don't need a husband."

"Yes, I do," she whined. "I need someone to take care of me."

86

I coughed because I wanted to be that man for her.

"You don't. As an independent mother and proprietress, you are doing well. You can do this, Violet."

When her eyes connected with mine, I longed to pull her into my arms and shield her from all her pain.

"You really think so?"

"I know so."

She finished the glass of water and set it aside before she stood. "Thank you, Zayne."

Then she retrieved a new pie from the pie safe.

"What's that for?"

"The mayor."

I frowned as I held the door open for her. "Why are you taking him a pie?"

She sighed heavily. "Because I promised to do so. And I don't think he'd like that one," she said as she pointed to the one being picked at by birds.

"Birds!" I yelled suddenly.

She laughed. "I see you've learned something from Will."

I placed my hand on the small of her back. "Let me walk with you."

"Oh, no. Surely it's out of your way."

"It's not. Isn't his office right up the street?"

She nodded. "But I promised I would bring it to his home."

"No. I don't think that's a good idea. Not after what you told me the other day. You need to deliver it to a very public place."

She stopped walking and turned to look at me. "You really think so?"

"Yes. I don't think you should trust him. Aren't you the one that said he wants what he can't have?"

Her shoulders sagged. "I said that."

"Then it's settled. I'm walking with you to deliver the pie to his office. I'll wait for you in a very visible place. If you're concerned, you just say my name and I'll be right there."

"Alright."

Right before we entered the town hall, she straightened her back and pasted a smile on her face. Then she led the way to the mayor's office. She asked him to speak to her in the hall.

When he arrived, he glared at me.

"I thought you were going to bring it by the house. And last week," Andrew Ward said.

"I was busy with the store." She thrust the pie toward him.

"I was hoping to talk to you alone." He took her arm and drew her a few paces away before he whispered something I could not hear.

When red colored her face, I stepped closer, but she raised her hand. She whispered harsh words to him, then turned on her heel. She strode toward me and looped her hand around my arm.

"The nerve!" she hissed. "Let's go."

"What did he say?" I asked.

"That he would divorce his wife and marry me!"

My gut clenched.

"Like I would give him the time of day. Not after how he hurt me. He chose *her* over me eight years ago. How could he think I would want him?"

I held the door of the town hall open for her. As we strode into the sunlight, I said, "See, you definitely don't need a husband."

She nudged my arm. "Certainly not one like him."

She took a deep breath and smiled.

"How was it leaving Eleanor this morning?"

I appreciated the change of topic as all the talk of husbands for Violet had me contemplating if I should put my hat in the ring. It would certainly solve a lot of her problems and one or two of my own.

"It was about as hard as I expected. Mama eventually pulled her from my arms and almost had to push me out the door."

"Well, looks like this is you," she said as we stopped in front of my office. "I won't keep you from your work any longer."

"Have a good day."

"Thanks, Zayne. It seems like I'm saying that a lot these days."

"Happy to help."

She smiled.

I watched as she walked back to her shop. The feelings I once had for her as a schoolboy had changed. Since coming back to Prescott, she wormed her way deeper into my heart. I loved her how a man loves the woman he wants to make his wife.

"Hey, if you're done gawking at the pretty lady," Al said as he poked his head out the door, "I've got time to show you around now."

Even though I went inside, back to my job, thoughts of Violet were never far from my mind.

CHAPTER 13

VIOLET

By the middle of July, my grief subsided some. I didn't have time to think about my broken heart. The pie shop kept me too busy. I hired another young lady named Zola Avery to help at the pie shop over the midday rush from eleven to four.

"Mmm. What smells so good?" Zola asked as she entered the kitchen one Friday, shortly before her shift.

"Beef stew."

"I wasn't expecting that."

"I'm adding a new pie to the menu for lunchtime, Colter Pot Pies. Made with real Colter beef," I said. "I'm hoping the savory offering will generate some lunchtime business with the locals."

"What an excellent idea!"

I showed Zola how to make the individually portioned pot pies. We baked four to start, so we could taste test them.

As we pulled them from the oven, a familiar male voice called from the front. "Hello, Violet!"

"Zayne, come on back."

I smiled as he greeted me with a kiss on my cheek. I liked he did that.

"You are about to become a test subject. Did you eat lunch yet?"

"No. And now that I've caught the delicious aroma in here, I'm starving." He laughed.

I really liked his laugh. In fact, I liked a lot of things about him. His smile. His attention. His kindness.

"Have a seat at the table." I pointed to the small table sitting in the kitchen's corner that we used on our breaks.

As I plopped the pot pie onto a plate for him, he took a seat. Then I handed him a spoon. Katie poured each of us coffee and slid the sugar bowl toward Zayne.

"I might spend too much time here since she knows how I take my coffee." He teased.

I set plates out for the rest of us before I took a seat next to him.

"It might be hot, so be careful."

He raised one eyebrow. "What is it?"

"One of my soon-to-be-famous Colter Pot Pies."

After he poked the spoon into the top of the overturned pie, thick stew oozed out of its crusty container. He used his spoon to break off a piece of crust and scoop up some of the stew filling. Then he blew on it for a second before he placed it in his mouth.

"Oh, that is good," he said with his mouth still full. His soft blue-gray eyes sparkled as he turned them toward me.

"Didn't your mother teach you not to speak with your mouth full?"

He swallowed. "I wasn't good at listening."

I snorted. "So, you like it?"

"I love it. You will be busy for the lunch hour once word gets around."

"It's not too salty?"

He reached for my hand and squeezed it. "It's as perfect as

the beautiful woman who created it."

Heat warmed my cheeks. Yes, I definitely liked a lot of things about Zayne Harrison.

"You should try it."

Katie, Zola, and I took bites of ours. It was even better than I hoped. Savory. Hearty. The beef melted in my mouth. The potatoes and carrots were too big for the pie, but perfect for a bowl of stew. I would dice those smaller for the next batch. Perhaps add a touch of rosemary.

"The crust holds up well. It's a little soggier than a traditional pie, but the texture goes well with the beef stew," Zola said. "It kind of reminds me of chicken and dumplings."

"Oh, we should make a chicken version too!" Katie suggested.

"Let's see if it succeeds. If it does, then I agree. We'll make a chicken one."

Zayne pulled out his pocket watch and stood. "I need to run."

"But you just got here."

He smiled. "Walk with me for a minute?"

I left the rest of my pot pie and placed my hand in the crook of his arm.

"I stopped to say hello on my way to the dock. We have a shipment arriving shortly. Thank you for lunch. That was amazing."

"I wish you could stay longer." And I truly did.

As we arrived near the docks, he stopped to face me. He let out a slow breath as his eyes searched mine.

"I really wish I could. But I must be off. Shall I stop by your house after supper tonight for a walk?"

"I would love that."

He leaned forward and kissed my cheek. "Until then, sweet Violet."

He turned and hurried away.

I walked back to the pie shop with a smile on my face and fluttery feelings in my heart. I could hardly wait until the evening.

When I returned to the pie shop, I quickly finished my pot pie, which tasted just as delicious, having sat for a few minutes. Then I joined Zola in preparing some apple pies for the afternoon train.

"I will make up a sign," Katie offered, "for the Colter Pot Pies."

"Splendid. I think Mama will love that I'm honoring her with the name."

"It's a brilliant idea. Especially since we are using beef. Locals are loyal to the brand."

During the rush of the afternoon train, Clinton Glassman stopped by. He asked me to meet him at his family's law office as soon as I could make the time that day. I wondered what he needed to talk to me about.

As soon as the rush slowed, Zola offered to stay until five and help Katie close up. I headed over to Glassman, Glassman, and Associates. I smiled at the sign and wondered which two Glassmans the name referred to.

When I entered the law office, the secretary showed me to Clinton's office.

"Good afternoon, Violet. Thanks for stopping by. Please, have a seat."

Clinton was a few years younger than me, but I remember-ed him from school. He had always been the studious sort. It did not surprise me he worked in his parents' law firm. After he took a seat, he ran a hand through his brown hair. His dark brown eyes softened.

"Keri asked me to look into Forest's estate. She mentioned no one had contacted you regarding the matter."

I straightened in my chair. I appreciated her asking her younger brother to look into it, as it never occurred to me I might need to deal with something. Mistakenly, I just assumed everything that was my late-husband's became mine.

"I have some good news and some bad news."

I cleared my throat. "Please go on."

"Forest had a life insurance policy. The terms of the policy show that the insurance company should have covered his final expenses."

"Oh. I paid for that out of our account. I didn't know."

"That is fine. We can still file the death certificate with the insurance company. They owe you one thousand dollars."

I took in a sharp breath of air. "So much?"

He smiled. "It was a modest policy, but still enough to cover your expenses."

A thousand dollars. That would allow me to set aside some money in savings for unexpected expenses.

"However," Clinton started. "I also discovered that the bank that Forest worked at holds a mortgage on your home."

I blinked. "I don't understand. He bought the house. Are you saying the bank owns my house?"

Clinton nodded. "It was a five-year loan with the last payment due at the end of August this year."

"But I haven't paid on any loans. I didn't know he had any."

"Be that as it may, the bank indicated you are behind for May through July. To bring the house payments current, you will need to pay the bank eight hundred dollars."

"Can I use the money from the life insurance?"

"It would be better to pay for it immediately. It might take several months to receive the funds from the insurance company."

I sighed heavily. "Will I lose my house?"

"That remains to be seen. Besides the eight hundred to bring your account current, you will have another two hundred for August, plus the balloon payment of one thou-sand five hundred."

I coughed as I did the math in my head. "That's two thousand and five hundred dollars that I need to find or I lose my house?"

Clinton's lips turned downward. "I'm sorry, Violet. I imagine this comes as a shock."

"A shock?" I rested my hand on my neck. "Of course it is a shock. I thought I owned my house. Now I might lose it."

He placed his hands flat on his desk.

"Is there anything else?"

"No. That was all I had to share."

"How much time do I have to pay?"

"Two weeks."

I slumped back against the chair as my head pounded. Two weeks. Two thousand five hundred dollars.

"Would you care for some water?"

I nodded numbly as the news sunk in. I knew James would loan me or even give me the money in a heartbeat. But I didn't want to ask him. He and Keri already did more than they should. I needed to do it myself.

Clinton offered me the water, and I drained the glass.

"I am happy to help with the paperwork or negotiations with the bank on your behalf, if you'd like."

"Thank you, Clinton."

I stood and left the building. As I walked home, the numbness settled over me. I did not know what to do.

Later that night, I was relieved when Zayne arrived with Eleanor a little earlier than normal.

"Where is Will?" he asked.

"Jaclyn is watching him. I need to talk to you with no distractions." I wrung my hands.

"What happened?"

As I closed the door behind me, I told him everything. He listened intently as we strolled to the nearby park. Then he suggested we sit on the bench.

"Do you have any savings?"

"I think we may have some, but I don't know. Since Forest passed, I have not gone through the books. I just paid the bills that showed up and I turned my attention to the pie shop to provide income."

"I would be happy to help you review the accounts, but only if you want my help. I know your family would help as well."

When Zayne slung his arm along the back of the bench, I scooted closer to his side and laid my head on his shoulder. He slid his arm around me. Sitting there with him, I did not feel so alone. Nothing had changed about my problem other than I shared it with him.

"I know I could ask James and he would make everything go away. But I'm tired of taking his charity. He and Keri have been overly generous. I want to fix this myself."

He rubbed his hand on my arm.

I turned to look at him. "What would you do?"

He kept his gaze facing forward. "I wouldn't advise you to do what I would."

Eleanor fussed, so I leaned forward and lifted her from the carriage. Then I held her close to my heart and leaned back against Zayne.

He cleared his throat. "You have several options. You could ask the bank to give you more time to pay. Let them know you're waiting for insurance money. That will cover what you owe them."

He paused for a moment. "One option is to let the house

go."

"Let the house go? Where will I live?"

"Even if you let it go, you'll have to pay eight hundred dollars for the missed payments. You could move in with James. I'm sure his offer still stands."

I frowned. "After all the times I refused to do so, I would feel foolish."

"Better to eat a slice of humble pie than overextend yourself."

I sighed. "I suppose you're right."

"You could also ask for his financial help, either charity or a loan, depending on what you are comfortable with."

When Eleanor fell asleep against me, I breathed deeply. I cherished her as much as her father.

Zayne removed his arm from around me and shifted his position to look at me. "You could move in with James until you found a new man to love. Then marry him."

My heart thrummed within my chest as his eyes studied mine. He reached up and traced his finger along my jawline. My breath caught as his face moved ever closer to mine.

"I think you know how fond I am of you," he whispered.

I stood abruptly. I wasn't ready to move on.

"Forest passed a few months ago. I'm carrying his child. I'm certain that is not what you want."

I kept my back facing him as I placed Eleanor in the carriage.

He stood and wrapped me in his arms. "Violet, I care for you regardless of your circumstances. I continue to hope that in time you will care for me, too."

I already did. But telling him only distracted me from my problems. It was not fair to saddle him with two more children, especially as he tried to rebuild his own life.

"I realize it is too soon for you to consider marriage

again." He stroked his hand on my hair. "So, I won't press you. Please promise me you will consider the option of living with your brother. It is a good option. You can pay your debts and have a little extra set aside while you get through the coming months of your pregnancy."

He released me and looked into my eyes again. "It would give you and I time to decide if the growing affection between us is something we both want to pursue."

Zayne smiled at me. "Regardless of what you decide, I would like to offer my help in reviewing your finances." He winked at me. "I am a businessman and have a great deal of experience managing accounts. If Monday night works for you, you could have supper at my house. Will that give you enough time to locate any records you have?"

"I think so."

"Good. Now, let me walk with you to pick up Will and then I'll see you home."

"Zayne?"

"Yes," he answered as we fell into step together.

"Thank you for everything."

He smiled, and my heart warmed. The notion of us as a couple was growing on me.

CHAPTER 14

ZAYNE

Sunday afternoon, I readied Eleanor in her carriage. Then I walked down the hill toward Violet's house. I knocked on the door and waited.

"Good evening." I smiled as she opened the door. "Ready for our walk?"

She greeted me and pulled the door closed.

"Forgetting someone?"

Her blue eyes sparkled as she laughed. "No. Will is out at the ranch. My nephew will drop him off in the afternoon tomorrow."

Violet placed her hand on the crook of my arm as I pushed Eleanor's carriage forward.

"Too bad. Eleanor will miss him."

She laughed again, and I treasured the sweet sound.

"I take it you are feeling better?"

"Yes. I hope I am over the worst of it."

"I'm looking forward to supper tomorrow night," I said.

She snorted. "Because you can hardly wait to see what a mess my finances are?"

"No. Because I finally get to share a meal with you at my home. Mama is very excited to know you better."

"She is?"

"Absolutely. I talk about you all the time. She's probably curious if you will live up to it."

We walked toward the park and slowed once we were in the shade.

She let out a long breath. "I found the records Forest kept, but I didn't look over them."

"That's fine. We'll review them tomorrow."

"I can't tell you how much I appreciate you, Zayne. You continue to help me and ask for nothing in return."

"Wait," I said as I winked at her. "I don't get pie from this arrangement?"

She giggled. "I suppose I could provide dessert for tomorrow night. What kind do you want?"

"Surprise me. I am happy to taste-test new things."

We bantered on as I turned the carriage back toward her house. When we arrived, I fought against my desire to kiss her. I wanted to give her time to grieve her loss. So, I settled for squeezing her hand and wishing her a good night.

———

The next morning, I bolted downstairs when I heard the telephone ring. I had barely finished shaving and was only half dressed.

"Hello?" I said into the mouthpiece.

"Zayne, it's Martin."

I held back a sigh.

"We need to talk about the situation in the Prescott office."

I frowned. "I'm not aware of a situation."

"Well, there is one. Can you catch the morning train down to Phoenix? Henry and I need to speak to you and his office is between Tucson and Prescott, so it makes sense for you and me to travel there."

"I..."

"Zayne, this is important. Surely Mama can watch Eleanor for a few days."

"A few days?"

"Well, overnight. We'll get you back to Prescott no later than tomorrow afternoon."

I would miss supper with Violet. That would upset her. She already had trust issues from her previous relationships. I didn't want to disappoint her.

"Zayne? Are you still there?"

"Yes, Martin. I will board the first train."

After I hung up the earpiece, I sighed. Then I darted back up the stairs and finished getting ready. I packed a few things for the night. Even though I hoped to come back that night, I thought it wise to prepare for the worst case.

When I finished, I penned a quick note to Violet, apologizing profusely for missing our date.

"Mama," I said as I hurried downstairs, "I don't know if I'll make it back tonight or not. I'll call either way."

"We'll take good care of Eleanor." She gave me a kiss on the cheek.

"Can you give this to Violet when she arrives for supper?"

"Oh, I completely forgot she was coming. Should I tell her to come another night?"

"If you don't mind welcoming her for supper, anyway. She should get to know you. If Jedediah is amenable, it might be nice if he could look over her finances. If not, I'll look on Wednesday."

"Don't worry about any of it. We will help her in any way we can."

"Thank you, Mama. I've got to hurry."

I planted a kiss on Eleanor's cheek and rushed out the door. I was still a half block away when the train whistle blew, so I ran to the ticket counter and quickly purchased a ticket. The train was already leaving the station by the time I sat down.

As trees whirred by, I hoped Violet would forgive me for missing supper with her. I knew her financial situation weighed heavily on her. Hopefully, Jedediah could provide her some guidance that would help ease her mind until I returned.

Once the train arrived in Phoenix, Henry greeted me on the platform.

"Zayne, good to see you again."

"Do you have any idea why Martin called this meeting?" I asked as I retrieved my handkerchief and blotted the perspiration from my forehead. It was insanely hot for the last leg of the train ride. The train station offered no reprieve.

"I do but will wait until Martin arrives to discuss it. He's going to take the streetcar when he gets here. Come, we'll head over for some lunch at the Adams Hotel."

When we stepped into the hotel, I was relieved that it seemed cooler than everywhere else. We sat at a table in the dining room.

"They have electric fans that blow air over enormous ice blocks," Henry explained. "The dining room is one of the nicer places to conduct business in the summer."

We ordered food and caught up on family happenings until Martin arrived.

As Martin approached, I mused over the fact that no one would ever guess we were brothers. I was tall and thin with sandy hair and blue eyes. Henry was a little rotund and short. His gray-streaked dark hair was thinning and his brown eyes always looked more menacing than they really were. Martin was quite tall and broad-shouldered. His thick, light brown hair held streaks of white. His gold eyes often hinted a smile was never far away. Though at the moment, a frown framed them. None of us looked even a little like each other.

"Martin." I stood and shook his hand. "We ordered you a sandwich."

"Excellent."

As soon as he sat down, he launched into his purpose.

"I understand that you have not assumed your duties as the general manager of the Prescott office."

"First, I've only been in town for a few weeks. I am still assessing the situation."

"Unacceptable."

"What Martin means to say," Henry interjected, "was that he wants to know more about your transition plan."

When the server brought our food, I took a big bite before responding.

"I planned to assess how the office runs and then, if adjustments are required, I will make them."

Martin frowned as he set his glass of iced tea down a little too hard on the table.

"You've had plenty of time to get over your loss and settle in. It's time for you to step up and contribute to the company."

My ire rose, and I clenched a fist under the table at his insinuation.

"As an equal partner, I have a say. I'm as educated as both of you and I understand business. Just because my approach differs from yours does not mean that I'm not contributing."

"Albert says that you have said nothing to him about taking over," Henry said.

"That is true. In fact, I plan to make him the permanent general manager."

"That is not your decision alone," Martin growled.

"Just as it was not your decision alone to make him the interim general manager. Yet, you did."

"Martin." Henry held up a hand to stop my brother's tirade.

"Look, Al has done an excellent job running the office. We should not demote him just because I arrived in town and I own part of the company. If he does great work, why not let him continue doing it?"

Henry asked what I had in mind as he shot Martin another warning look.

"We need to consolidate a few activities. We should handle our rate negotiations at the company level and not for each individual location. Since all our offices work with the various railroads now, it makes sense to negotiate contracts across the board. Why should we have one rate for freight shipped from Prescott and a different one for Verde Valley, even if the distances are the same?"

Martin relaxed a little, though he said nothing and focused on eating his meal.

"I also think we should manage freight claims centrally. We could develop relationships with each of the railways and their claims departments. If we had a few people managing that, the railways would have a consistent contact."

"I like it. So are there other centralized activities you were considering?" Henry asked.

"That's it. We could try out those first. I could start the process and if we need more staff, I could hire. We have empty offices in the new building. I can take over those."

After Martin pushed his plate away, he rubbed a hand on his chin. "Your idea has merit."

That was a tremendous compliment coming from him.

"I see it could be the beginning of a corporate office,"

Henry said.

Martin frowned. "Would we want to headquarter in Prescott, though?"

"Why not?" I argued. "We can ship interoffice paperwork through the train for express delivery. So it doesn't really matter if the centralized activities are in Tucson, Phoenix, or Prescott."

"Yes, but if we increase the number of centralized activities, like adding a centralized billing department, then we may want that in Phoenix. It is the territorial capital now."

"I don't think that really makes a difference," I argued.

We spent the next few hours weighing our options. Eventually, Martin and Henry agreed to let me start the centralized operations in Prescott with the caveat that we may move it later. Since it was my idea, they thought it was best if I managed it. We also agreed to come up with a list of centralized activities and a priority that we would discuss at our next regularly scheduled partner's meeting.

When we finished, I made a telephone call up to Mama to let her know I would not make it home until tomorrow afternoon. She promised to take care of Violet for me.

Unfortunately, it was almost suppertime when we concluded our business. Henry drove us to his house for the meal.

As the night wore on, his wife set up guest beds on the veranda. I was skeptical about sleeping outside at first, until I learned the entire family did through the summer.

"How do you endure days on end of this heat?" I asked as Henry showed us to our beds.

"It is difficult. You'll want to dip the sheet in the bucket of water by the bed," Henry instructed. "It will keep you cool at least long enough to fall asleep."

I stripped down to my underthings, especially since his wife and children were on the other end of the veranda, separated from us by a curtain. Then I dipped the sheet in the water and wrung it out before laying it loosely over me.

Regardless of the wet blanket, I still found the heat oppressive. As I failed to fall asleep, I resolved we would not move the centralized services to Phoenix. There was no way I would move there or drag Violet and our children there.

Once that thought popped into my mind, I dreamed of a home with her, me, Eleanor, Will, and baby Gamble. It warmed my heart and helped me fall asleep to pleasant dreams.

CHAPTER 15

VIOLET

Monday afternoon, I vacillated between excitement and dread. The thought of sharing a meal with Zayne and his parents pleased me. The thought of what horrible secrets lie in the financial books terrified me.

Will squirmed out of my grip as we climbed the front porch stairs to Zayne's home. The porch swept the entire length of the large house. A few groupings of wicker chairs and side tables made the porch more inviting.

"Stay here," I warned my son as I knocked on the door.

"Good evening, Mrs. Gamble," a rotund young woman with light brown hair greeted me. Her cheeks were rosy and her brown eyes lit with excitement when she saw Will.

"This is the young Master Gamble?"

"Master," Will parroted back before he giggled.

"Please come in. I am Miss Harmony, the nanny and housekeeper. Should I take Master Gamble to the playroom while you wait for supper?"

As I stepped into the parlor, I barely kept my jaw from slacking. The home was even larger than I thought and so ornately decorated. I couldn't imagine children living there.

When Miss Harmony cleared her throat, I finally answered, "Yes, please."

She bent down to Will's level. "What say you to some fun upstairs? I have wooden blocks and logs to build a cabin."

"Blocks!" Will clapped his hands together in excitement. Miss Harmony took his hand and led him upstairs.

"Ah, Mrs. Gamble," a man greeted me from the other end of the parlor. "Let me take your things."

The man had thick salt and pepper hair atop his rather narrow head. His dark eyes were kind. He was thin and only slightly taller than me, not anywhere near Zayne's height.

"I'm Mr. Cole, but you may call me Jedediah."

"Thank you, Jedediah. I brought some of my chocolate cream pie for dessert."

"Grace will be pleased to hear it, as your pie is the envy of the town."

He took the pie and ledgers from my hand before he set the ledgers on a side table. Then he set the pie in the dining room. The parlor housed several couches and wingback chairs throughout. Small, dark wood tables sat between the various groupings. A large marble fireplace stood along one wall. The home boasted wealth without being overly flamboyant.

"Mrs. Gamble," Grace Cole greeted me. She was short and her blond hair held streaks of gray along the edges. Her eyes were mirror images of Zayne's.

I wondered why he hadn't shown up.

"Please call me Violet."

"Zayne sends his regrets. He had a last-minute partners' meeting in Phoenix this morning. He barely made it to the train on time. But he left this for you."

She held out an envelope. "Please have a seat to read it. Supper will be finished shortly."

I thanked her, then I slid my finger underneath the flap of the envelope. My heart raced as I fought against the feelings of abandonment from past suitors. It hurt that Zayne was not there. I sniffed to hold back my tears while I read his note.

Dearest Violet,

It breaks my heart that I could not keep my promise to help you this evening. Unfortunately, I was called away for an emergency partners' meeting this morning. I would have stopped by the shop to explain, but there was no time.

I know you feel hurt by my broken promise, so I will remind you it was not my intent.

My mother and Jedediah still wanted to entertain you this evening. I thought you might like to know them better. They are good and kind people, so I know you will enjoy the evening.

Jedediah has agreed to help you review the books in my absence. He is the chief financial officer of the railway, so I couldn't find a better stand-in. I think you will find his knowledge and advice quite useful.

Again, sweet Violet, I am sorry to miss the evening with you. My heart is there, even though I cannot be.

Yours,

Zayne

I blinked away tears that threatened to spill over. He wrote to me. He was the first man to do so, and I was grateful for it. His words eased my anxiety and fear about his regard for me and about dining without him.

I folded the note and placed it in my reticule.

"Supper is ready," Grace said as she came over to me. "Was my son duly apologetic?"

I nodded.

"Good. He was more upset about breaking off the plans with you than about leaving Eleanor."

"That can't be." I smiled. "I know how he adores her."

Grace laughed as she led me into the dining room. After we sat down, Jedediah blessed the meal.

Grace said, "Thank you so much for bringing your award-winning pie. I've been meaning to stop by your shop for a piece. Zayne raves about it."

I laughed. "Does he? Sometimes he eats it so fast, I wonder he tastes it."

She served me some roast, potatoes, carrots, and parsnips. The aroma of rosemary and garlic wafted up to my nose.

"This smells delicious."

Her cheeks flushed. "Thank you. It was the first meal that Zayne's father taught me how to cook. I'll admit to being rather nervous knowing that such an accomplished baker was coming to my home. I almost asked our cook to switch her night off."

I took a bite, and the roast beef melted in my mouth. When I swallowed it, I reassured her. "You have nothing to fear. This is quite tender and the flavors balance perfectly."

"Thank you. I hope you don't mind, but I sent a plate upstairs for Harmony to feed your son."

"Not at all. It is nice not to be distracted for one meal. If memory serves, you raised a rather large family?"

"Yes. Fourteen in all. Seven girls and seven boys."

"All adopted?" I asked.

"All except Zayne. He was our only natural born child. Though if you ask him, he will confirm that he did not receive any special treatment. Sometimes I think Joshua was harder on him than his brothers."

The conversation flowed as we ate the meal. Jedediah

spoke about his children from his first marriage. His wife passed when his children were teenagers, so by the time he met Grace, they were grown.

"How did the two of you meet?" I asked.

Grace blushed. "Well, it is an unusual story. Jedediah moved into the house next door. When Joshua passed, he heard the commotion and came by to see what happened."

Jedediah squeezed her hand as she dabbed at a few tears.

"In the weeks and months that followed, he stopped by to check on me. Having lost his dear wife, he was very empathetic."

He laughed. "The next thing I knew, my youngest daughter was baking cookies for me to bring over as an excuse. I think she knew I was falling in love with Grace and wanted to help me along."

Grace smiled. "It was hard to say exactly when I fell in love with Jedediah. We became such good friends. He helped me through the most difficult time of my life. Within months of Joshua's passing, the last of my children moved out. So they left me alone in this big, empty house. Had it not been for Jedediah's friendship, I might have fallen into a deep despair."

He said he remembered the first time he asked to kiss her. "You asked me why I would want to."

She laughed. "I was just so surprised that we fell in love without realizing it. I didn't know until that first kiss."

"How long after Zayne's father passed did you marry?"

"I think it was around six months. Some folks thought that was too soon, of course. But they didn't know our hearts. There was nothing wrong with a widower and a widow moving on."

I frowned. A widower, Zayne. A widow, me.

Just like Grace and Jedediah, I relied on Zayne's friendship. We had become close friends, but I was not sure when or how. I welcomed seeing him again. I might even love him.

I took a sip of my iced tea to chase away the thoughts. My heart still judged me. It was too soon to forget Forest. Wasn't it?

"Would you rather have some pie or wait for supper to settle?"

"Can we wait a bit?"

"Absolutely. Let me clear the dishes away. Jedediah, would you like to review Violet's ledgers?"

He nodded and stood. Once he retrieved them, he sat at the table again.

I stood and helped Grace clear the dishes away.

"Oh, you don't have to help."

"I want to. No need to leave you to clean this all on your own. If you wash, I'll dry them."

Grace smiled as she filled the washbasin with warm water from the sink. "Your mother did a fine job raising you."

"Do you know my mother?"

"Of course. Who doesn't know Will and Hannah Colter? Though I wish I would have known her better when we were young mothers."

"I suppose raising so many rowdy boys gave you much in common."

Grace laughed.

"May I ask you a question? I'm afraid it is rather forward of me to do so."

"Certainly," I replied.

"When is your baby due?"

I sighed heavily. "Mid-November, if I calculated correctly."

"So your late husband didn't even know?"

A lone tear slid down my cheek. I wiped it away with my hand. "No. I was so consumed with my loss that I didn't even realize it until the morning sickness came."

"And has that subsided at all?"

"Mostly. Enough that I can open the shop in the morning."

She handed me a plate, which I took and dried.

"You are an incredibly brave woman, Violet. Choosing independence for yourself and your son is a tough thing. I admire you."

"Thank you. Although, my independence may come to a close if I can't keep my house."

She handed me the last dish. I dried it and set it aside.

"I will put those away later. Come, let's have some pie while we talk about your future."

She dished up three pieces. I carried one for myself and Jedediah into the dining room. Then I went to the kitchen and poured us coffee. Grace carried her coffee and pie while I brought the two cups of coffee.

"Thank you, Violet."

"So, what do you think?" I asked as I took a bite of pie.

"Well, it does not appear that you have enough funds in your accounts to come up with the large balloon payment."

"As I feared."

He took a bite of pie. His eyes rounded. "This is so creamy. I've never tasted such delicious chocolate before."

I smiled.

"I can see why you won first prize," Grace said. "It is the best pie I've ever tasted."

"Thank you."

"Regarding the balloon payment, I doubt the bank will give you an extension or another loan to cover it. Even if they did, I would advise against it. You are better off living with family than overextending yourself with a child on the way."

"That was what Zayne thought."

Grace smiled. "He is getting wiser in his old age."

I smiled.

"We know how unpredictable delivering a child can be," Jedediah said, as his face turned red.

"Yes. Zayne's wife lost several children before Eleanor," Grace said. "And I assume you know what happened."

I nodded.

"We would hate to see you stretch your finances so thin and place an undue burden on yourself to earn more at the shop."

"Well said, Grace. It looks like your income at the shop covers your monthly expenses well enough. Though I think it would be put to better use saving for your child."

I sighed. "So I should give up my home?"

"I know it is hard," Grace said as she reached across the table for my hand. "You can rely on your family in town to help you. So, don't take on debt to keep a roof over your head. In the long run, it will be better for you."

"Then once the child has arrived and you've built up savings, you can purchase your own home without carrying extra debt."

"Or," Grace said with a smile, "You may not need to purchase a home if you were to marry again."

"Do I have to pay the back payments?"

"Yes, but the bank should work with you since you are expecting money from the life insurance."

"I suppose I ought to grovel at James's feet, then."

Jedediah cleared his throat. "Working with him as I do, you only have to let him know you are in need."

"Thank you both for your advice and for looking over my finances. And for the lovely evening. I should take Will home and put him to bed now."

They rang for Harmony, and she brought my sleepy-eyed

son down. I retrieved my books and said my farewells before walking down the hill.

Once at home, with Will in bed, I sat in my favorite chair in the parlor. Perhaps it was best to let the house go. It contained so many memories of Forest. At least James's house held no sad memories for me. They had the space and a nanny to help. My mornings would be less hectic since I could leave Will with the nanny and head directly to the pie shop.

Perhaps Zayne and his parents were right. I should accept James's hospitality and ease my burden.

CHAPTER 16

ZAYNE

When I returned to Prescott late the next afternoon, I stopped by the pie shop before it closed, eager to see Violet. Since a large crowd gathered from the train, I found a table to wait for them to clear out. As soon as the last person in line ordered, I hurried to the counter.

Katie greeted me with a warm smile. "Mr. Harrison. I'm sure Violet will want to know you're back. Just one second."

She dashed off to the kitchen and quickly returned with Violet in tow.

"Hello." Violet smiled when she saw me. My, how I loved her smiles. They warmed me from head to toe.

"Are you able to take a break?" I asked.

"Of course. Here, try this one."

"Citrus pie." It looked new, and it piqued my curiosity. She handed me a plate, then brought two cups of coffee and some sugar.

"So, what's in this?" I asked.

Violet grinned. "Humor me, Zayne. Taste it and tell me."

I used the fork to cut off a bite. Then I let it roll around on my tongue. So creamy. Tangy citrus blended with the sweet cream flavor.

"Orange and lemon," I said with confidence.

"And?" She raised an eyebrow.

"There's more?"

She nodded.

"Lime?"

"Can you taste it, or did you just guess?"

"I guessed. The flavors blend well. It's very good."

"Thank you."

As Violet sipped her coffee, I sheepishly asked, "You are not angry at me for missing supper?"

When she let out a sigh, she glanced toward the train platform. Then she met my gaze. "Not really. I appreciated your note."

Even though she seemed hesitant, I breathed a little easier.

"I'm glad. I'll admit I was worried you might not speak to me again."

She gave me a small smile and a wink. "Wouldn't want to lose one of my best customers."

A laugh escaped from my mouth before I ate another bite of the fluffy pie. "How was supper with my parents?"

"Your mother and Jedediah were a tremendous help. I really like your mother. She is so nice. I really enjoyed our visit."

"Good. I knew she would take care of you."

"And it thrilled her I brought the chocolate pie. I didn't know she wanted some or I would have sent some home with you sooner. I'm not sure they left any for you."

I chuckled. "I know where to find more."

Once I finished the last bite, I complimented her on the pie. "That was perfectly refreshing after an overly warm trip."

"Phoenix was hotter than here?"

"Significantly hotter. I will take an extra set of everything when I travel down there during the summer."

Violet looked down at her coffee and her jovial expression turned serious. I wanted to take care of her, protect her, help her with all her worries, and make her life easier. She had wormed her way back into my heart so quickly and deeply. I didn't think I would fall in love again after losing Rose. Yet, sitting there with Violet, I thought I may have always loved her. The confusing thoughts were hard to reconcile and sometimes made me feel guilty, as if allowing myself to love Violet diminished what I felt for Rose.

"Zayne, are we courting?"

I swallowed a sip of coffee as I pondered her question. At that moment, I realized she was everything I wanted for my future. I wanted an official courtship with her. One that led to a lifetime together.

"Would you like that?"

She took a sip and studied me for several seconds. "I think so. Would you? Would you rather run away from a widow with two children?"

My heart squeezed tight. I would still want her if she had ten children. None of that deterred me. Perhaps I was like my father, ready to love any children that came with the most important woman in my life.

"Not at all. It would honor me to court you. But you realize the intent of courting?"

"Of course." She lowered her head and glanced up at me as her cheeks reddened.

"And that doesn't scare you away?"

"Promise no more pranks?"

I laughed. "I will gladly promise that. Especially since I've learned so many other ways to coax a smile from you."

She raised an eyebrow. "Oh?"

"You are the prettiest woman at the train station."

Those lovely blue eyes sparkled as she smiled, and pink

settled on the apples of her cheeks again.

I winked at her. "See, I can learn new tricks."

After she finished her coffee, she stood. "Well, I need to make my plan for tomorrow. I'm sure you are ready to head home to see Eleanor."

"Perhaps you would join me for supper tomorrow night at my house. I promise to be there this time."

"I would love to."

Then I stood and pulled her into my arms. She smelled like oranges, probably from making the citrus pies. After she wrapped her arms around me, she stretched up to kiss me on the cheek.

"I missed you," I whispered as I reluctantly let her go. Oh, how I wanted to give her a proper kiss. It would leave no doubt in her mind how much she meant to me.

She slipped out of my hold and smiled. "See you tomorrow."

Goodness alive. I loved her smile.

————

The next evening, I walked down to Violet's house to escort her up the hill. When I knocked on her door, I heard Will whining. I waited patiently for her to answer.

"Oh, hi."

The pale blue dress, not widow's black, brought out the blue in her eyes. The long flowing material highlighted her pleasing figure while minimizing her condition, stealing away my breath. Her twisted lips weren't the expression I had hoped for in a greeting, but a quick glance at Will's shoes in her hand confirmed my bad timing.

I smiled as I handed her a bouquet and entered the house. She rewarded me with a half-smile as she took them.

"What's the matter?"

She let out a frustrated growl. "Someone doesn't want to wear his shoes."

"May I?"

She thrust the pair of shoes toward me. Then she turned to retrieve a vase and water for the flowers. As she absent-mindedly arranged the flowers, she watched me.

"Hey there, little man."

"Zay!" Will jumped up from the floor and ran toward me. Then he hugged my leg.

"What's this about not putting your shoes on?"

His cute little lower lip protruded. "Don't want to."

"Aren't you hungry?"

"Yup."

"Well, to have supper at my house, you must wear your shoes. You're too big for your mama to carry you every-where."

"See Miss Mony?"

I quirked an eyebrow and glanced at Violet.

"He means Miss Harmony."

"Yes."

"K." He sat down and pointed at his feet.

I sat on the floor next to him and put his shoes on. As soon as I tied his laces, he jumped up.

"See Mony!"

As I stood, I chuckled at his excitement. Violet joined me. "Ready?"

She nodded.

As we walked up the street, I held Will's hand. Violet slipped her hand into the crook of my other arm.

"You look lovely in that dress," I said.

"Thank you. You don't look so bad yourself."

I snorted. "Not dashing?"

"Hmm. Maybe handsome."

She nudged my arm. Her playful teasing made me smile.

When Miss Harmony opened the door to my home, Will launched himself at her. She lifted him into her arms and carried him upstairs, asking him questions about his day.

"I guess she made more of an impression than I thought," Violet said.

"Violet," my mother greeted her. "You look beautiful this evening."

She handed Mama the pie she brought.

"Oh, is this something new?"

"Citrus cream pie," I said. "I had a piece yesterday. It's good."

Violet's cheeks turned rosy at the compliment. After Jedediah greeted Violet, Mama led us into the dining room. We took our seats, and Mama served the meal.

"The cook discovered this new dish. It's called Chicken Tetrazzini. I hope you enjoy it."

As we ate, Violet started the conversation.

"I spoke with James this morning when I dropped off Will. He was thrilled about me moving in. He promised to get the rooms ready this weekend. A nursery adjoins the nanny's room, and he thought Will could have it. There is another room on the other side."

"That's good news!" Mama exclaimed.

Though I was happy Violet's brother would provide for her, a part of me wished she could move into my home. Become my wife. Let me be her provider. Unfortunately, I could not until we were married, and I figured she needed more time to get used to the idea.

"I will have to go through Forest's stuff. I've been avoiding it."

"It took me a long time to part with Rose's things. I doubt

I would have if I had not moved here."

"Until now, it seemed easier to leave everything where it was. I think moving will help me let go more. It's hard to be in the house reminded of him all the time."

Mama agreed. "Staying in this house was hard. It took a long time before I could go through the house without thinking of Zayne's father."

Jedediah squeezed Mama's hand. He was so patient with her and so generous to have moved into our family home. It must have been hard for him.

"Will you move into James's house this weekend?" I asked.

"Probably not until next weekend. I'm sure he'll rope all my brothers into helping."

"I will, of course, be happy to help."

"Thank you."

When there was a lull, I shared with her my plans for the freight company. She listened intently as I described my approach and goals. I liked that she seemed genuinely interested in my work.

Following dessert, we retired to the parlor. I led her to the couch. As she settled on it, she asked, "Would it be completely inappropriate for me to ask for a stool to prop up my feet?"

"Not at all." I moved the coffee table further away from the couch. Then I slid a footstool in front of her before I sat next to her.

She sighed contentedly as she propped her feet on it. "I could get used to this."

My heart agreed. I could get used to her in my home, on my couch, and by my side. Forever would be about long enough.

When she rested her arm across my middle and snuggled closer, I laid my arm on her shoulders. Her hair smelled like vanilla and citrus. I inhaled deeply, wishing again to never leave her company.

After several minutes, her arm went slack, and her breathing softened.

"I think she's asleep," Mama whispered. "You should probably walk her home."

I glanced at the clock. It was half past seven, but I couldn't bring myself to wake her. "Soon."

Mama smiled. She knew how much I cared for Violet.

"Oh. I'm so sorry," Violet said a few minutes later. "I think I fell asleep."

I chuckled softly. "You did, but that's alright."

"I should really get Will home and to bed."

She slid away from me, and I missed her already.

"Let me fetch Harmony." Mama rang a bell. "She'll be down shortly."

After Harmony appeared with a sleeping Will in her arms, I stood. "Here, I'll take him."

Harmony carefully plied Will from her shoulder and helped me get him settled against my chest. She handed Violet his shoes.

"Good night, Master Will." She placed a kiss on his cheek. "He is such a precious little boy."

Violet snorted. "That's because you've never seen him in the morning."

Harmony laughed. "I would still feel the same."

I held Will with one arm and extended my hand to Violet. She took it and interlaced her fingers with mine. After Mama and Jedediah said their farewells, I led her to the front door. We walked down the hill in silence.

When we arrived at her house, she asked to take Will from me, but I refused. "Let me take him upstairs."

She turned on the lamp. Then she led the way upstairs to his room. She flicked on the electric overhead light.

"Just lay him on the bed. I won't try to change him out of his clothes. Don't want to wake him."

After she pulled back the covers, I gently lowered him to the bed. As she tucked him in, my breath caught. Not only did I love her, but I loved her little boy, too.

I leaned over and placed a kiss on his cheek. "Good night, little man."

Violet sniffed as she escorted me back downstairs. She wiped her hand across her cheek.

"What's wrong?" I asked as I faced her.

"Nothing. Absolutely nothing."

Then I rested my hands on her waist, and she looped her arms behind my neck. I breathed deeply and caught the faint citrus smell I noticed earlier. She was so beautiful.

"You are so good with him," she whispered.

"Thank you. I had a superb role model."

"You must miss him."

"Very much."

As I studied her bright blue eyes, I cleared my throat. "May I kiss you?"

She nodded.

Then I lowered my lips and gently brushed them across hers. She tasted sweet, like that citrus pie. Even though I wanted to kiss her much longer, I slowed the kiss, intending to pull away. When her hand slid behind my neck, she returned my kiss. I eagerly tasted her lips again while I pressed her closer, deepening the kiss. Slowly, I ended the kiss and leaned back. My heart hammered against my chest when she remained in my embrace, making no move to leave.

"Zayne?"

"Hmm?"

"Will you kiss me again?"

Of course, I gladly obliged the woman of my dreams.

CHAPTER 17

VIOLET

Zayne's first kiss awakened a deeper interest in me. When he pulled his lips away from mine, I could not bring myself to part from his company. Not after his gentle suggestion of how he felt about me. I wanted another kiss from the man who worked his way into my heart.

"Will you kiss me again?"

The words barely escaped before his lips crashed over mine again. I leaned into his embrace and strength. His hand moved from my low back to my neck and hair, stoking a desire in me I never expected to feel again. I returned his kiss with an urgency that surprised me.

He pulled away abruptly.

"Violet."

He said my name with such longing and tenderness, leaving no doubt in my mind that he loved me. Truly loved me. I slid my hands down his arms, ready to step away, but his hands remained on my waist, and I stopped.

"I love you," he said with a husky voice.

As my pulse raced, I held my breath. I was not ready for such declarations. The feelings rushing to my heart confused me. I felt strongly about Zayne. Yet, memories of Forest tried to push forward. I loved my husband with all my heart. Didn't I?

"I'm sorry."

He released his hold on me and my legs felt wobbly.

"I know. You're not ready. I can see it on your face, Violet."

Tears burned my eyes. I looked at the corner of the room, sorry to disappoint him. He gave me the gift of his love. I thought I was ready to accept it, but I wasn't.

"Vi, look at me."

He placed his finger under my chin and gently directed my gaze towards him. "I understand better than you think. It's alright."

The moisture from my eyes spilled over to my cheeks. Then his thumb caressed away my tears before he drew me into his arms for a hug. I wrapped my arms around his middle, relieved that he understood me.

After a minute, he kissed my forehead. He let out a long breath while sliding his hands down my arms. Then he squeezed my hands and released them before he stepped backward.

"Good night, Violet."

I cleared my throat. "Good night."

Then he left. I closed the door behind him and locked it before I rested my forehead against it.

At that moment, I thought I loved two men. My late husband and Zayne.

———

A week and a half later, I looked around the house. Tomorrow was moving day, and I had absolutely nothing packed.

I lifted the earpiece from the telephone and asked for Jaclyn's home.

"Hello?"

"Jaclyn? It's me. Vi."

"Hello!" The excitement in her voice encouraged me.

"Do you have some trunks or crates? I have nothing packed. Not a single thing."

"Oh. Let me check with Boone. We may have some at the office. Then I'll be over, if you'd like some help."

"Thank you."

I hung up the telephone before I looked around downstairs. Just as I started up the stairs, the telephone rang. I hurried over to it.

"Vi?"

"Hello, Justine."

"Would you like my help?"

Clearly, Jaclyn had called her immediately after hanging up with me.

"Yes, that would be nice."

"Do you want me to see if Grady would mind watching Will? He could sleep overnight at my place."

I thought for a moment. It would make packing easier. "That's a good idea."

"Great. We'll be over soon."

"The door will be open. I'll be upstairs."

"Alright. See you soon."

When the line clicked, I replaced the earpiece in its cradle. Then I climbed the stairs and packed a small bag for Will. I brought him and the bag into my room.

Forest's wardrobe loomed in front of me. I swallowed hard, tempted to ask my brothers to take it unopened to some charity. No. I wanted to go through it. See if there was anything I wanted to keep for Will.

I took a few steps toward the large piece of furniture and eyed it like it might attack me any minute. Nope. Not ready. Instead, I veered off to Forest's nightstand. Best to start small and work my way up to the harder tasks.

As I sat on the edge of the bed, I opened the drawer on his nightstand and picked up his Bible. Tears formed instantly as I ran my hand over the soft leather. I opened the front cover and read the dedication.

"To our son, Forest, on your eighteenth birthday. May His Word light your path. Love, Mama and Papa."

I choked on a sob. Then I bit my lower lip to hold it at bay.

When I turned the page, my heart plummeted. A photograph of a young woman slipped from the pages and fluttered to the floor. I glared at the photograph for a minute. My stomach tightened. My heart ached. It looked nothing like his mother. He had no sisters.

As I leaned down to retrieve it, my hand shook. Will babbled as he played with his blocks, entirely unaware of the fear crushing my heart like a vise.

When my fingers connected with the corner of the photograph, my eyes blurred. I lifted the woman's likeness from the floor.

"Oh, Forest. Who was she to you?"

I hoped a name on the back would quiet the whispers of betrayal. My shoulders slumped. No name. Only an address and a note. I held it closer to the lamp on the nightstand.

"Born 1881."

I frowned. I was born in 1878. Forest was a few years older than me. So, who was this mystery younger woman?

"Violet!" Justine's voice at the bottom of the stairs startled me.

I quickly stuffed the picture back into the cover of his Bible. Then I dropped it back into its hiding place and slammed the drawer shut. I couldn't stop shaking. I wasn't sure if it was from heartbreak or rage.

"Oh, Vi," Justine said the moment she saw me. "I'm so glad we came to help. This must be so hard."

She sat next to me on the edge of the bed. When she wrapped her arms around me, I let the sobs come. Grady picked up Will and the bag I set out for him before he left without a word. Justine believed my breakdown was grief over losing Forest and not from a spirit crushed his secret.

By the time Jaclyn arrived, I calmed enough to be useful. She and Boone brought several crates and trunks upstairs.

"Do you want to keep any of Forest's clothing?" Justine asked.

"No. If you come across his watch, cuff links, and other keepsakes, I want to save them for Will."

"Alright. I'll work on his wardrobe. Anything I have questions about, I'll set out on the bed for you to decide."

"Thank you."

"Why don't we pack up Will's room?" Jaclyn suggested.

I nodded numbly as I followed her into Will's room. We made quick work of packing it up, since his things fit into one trunk.

While Jaclyn chatted with me, my mind kept going back to the photograph in Forest's Bible. I wondered who the woman could be. Was it a former sweetheart that he had never mentioned?

The address. It looked familiar. It was a street address in Prescott.

Could she be a lover?

The thought doubled me over. I moaned, and Jaclyn rushed to my side.

"Are you alright? Here, sit on Will's bed for a moment. Is

it the baby?"

I shook my head. "I'm just a little tired."

Jaclyn raised an eyebrow. "I think you're overdoing it. We're done in here. Lay down for a few minutes. I can pack your wardrobe. Is there a particular dress you want for tomorrow?"

"Just one of the brown work dresses."

"Rest for a few minutes. Justine and I will start in the kitchen after we finish your room."

I nodded as she closed the door behind her. Then I curled up in a ball and hugged Will's pillow to my chest.

"Forest. What have you done?" A sob choked off more words.

Instead, my mind cataloged any strange behavior over the years. I came up short. He never stayed late at work. He never went out without me unless it was with one of his friends or my brothers. They usually met at our house and left together. He never avoided me. Nothing stood out as signs of...

As I tried to make sense of something that didn't make sense, my heart withered. Exhaustion pulled at me.

Neither Jaclyn nor Justine bothered me. When I woke up a few hours later, the house was dark, and the front door was locked. Stacks of crates lined both sides of the door. The smaller stack was the items for donation. The other was our kitchen things and my clothes.

I climbed the stairs again and entered my bedroom. A crate sat on the bed, so I rummaged through it. Forest's watch. His cuff links. His Bible. Some photographs of his family.

Then I frowned and paid closer attention to the photographs. I retrieved the one of the mystery woman and compared it to the faces of his family. She didn't look like any of them.

I wanted to hope she was a distant relation, but I couldn't deny the obvious answer. I opened my Bible and stuffed her image in the front. I would leave his things packed up once I moved in with James and Keri. But I wanted that photograph handy until I solved the mystery.

Then I changed into a nightgown and slid under the covers, crying myself to sleep over my late husband's betrayal.

The next morning, I woke early and dressed for the day. I skipped breakfast, and I packed up the remaining things before my family arrived. All my brothers that lived locally showed up, even Sam and Deacon who lived at the ranch. Zayne arrived a few minutes later.

As they started loading things in the wagon, Zayne pulled me away from the commotion.

"Morning." His smile dimmed when I looked away.

"What's wrong?" he asked.

"Nothing."

He tried to pull me close for a hug, but I pushed him away. Nothing could comfort my broken heart.

"I said nothing, alright!"

He frowned and studied me for a minute. "Are you upset with me?"

I glared at him. "Not everything in this world revolves around you, Zayne."

Then I stormed away as I saw the look of hurt on his face.

When I tried to lift a crate, Deacon took it from me.

"Not a chance, Vi. You're limited to packing and unpacking. No lifting."

I rolled my eyes. "You're a vet, not a doctor."

"He's right," Sam said. "Mama made us promise not to let you lift a thing. She was feeling under the weather, so she's trusting us to watch out for you."

I huffed as I slouched into a chair at the table.

"Hey, what are we doing with the furniture?" Boone asked.

"It stays. The bank agreed to reduce the amount I owed them if I left the furniture. The only thing we're taking is my wardrobe."

"Yes, ma'am."

He cajoled Grady to go with him upstairs to bring down the heavy piece of furniture.

Zayne glanced at me each time he entered the house for another crate or trunk. After his third trip, I mouthed the words, "I'm sorry." He winked at me, and his step seemed lighter after that.

When we arrived at James's house, he directed as the others unloaded. He told my brothers to put the household goods in the storage shed.

"It's weatherproof, so even if you have keepsakes, they will be fine," he reassured me.

When Zayne and Boone carried the wardrobe to my room, I followed behind and started unpacking my trunk.

"Hey," Zayne said. "If you want to talk about what is bothering you, I can stay."

"Nothing is wrong." I lifted my chin.

He frowned.

"Is this because of the other night?"

I frowned. "No."

He held my gaze until I looked away. The last thing I wanted was to tell the new man in my life about the foibles of my late husband.

"Vi," he whispered. "Please don't push me away."

"Zayne, let me be. The last few days have been taxing. It's been much harder than I expected. I just need some space."

"Fine." His terse response pierced my heart.

I knew my silence hurt him. But I could not deal with the

mystery woman, Forest's passing, and Zayne's feelings right then.

He stormed out of the room. Sam also hurried from the room when he saw my expression.

I sighed. I was being a terrible sister. So, I tossed aside a dress and marched down the stairs. Until my brothers and Zayne finished unloading the wagon, I hovered. Then I pasted on a barely sincere smile and thanked each of them for their help.

"I'll take the donation items to the church for distribution," Boone said as he side-hugged me.

"And I'll send Justine over with Will soon," Grady said.

"Thank you. I really appreciate everything."

After the rest of my brothers hugged me, Zayne approached. He leaned forward and kissed my cheek. "See you at church tomorrow?"

My eyes burned. I nodded. "Thank you."

He smiled. "Of course."

When they left, I quickly unpacked Will's things. Then I hid in my room until supper under the guise of unpacking. I needed more time to process what the picture meant to my late husband.

CHAPTER 18

ZAYNE

When I arrived Saturday morning to help Violet move, I expected her to be a little sullen. Surely, going through her late husband's things pained her. However, it did not prepare me for the icy glares she directed my way. The wall she erected between us tore at my heart.

After those kisses and my declaration of love the previous week, I barely saw her. She was busy the two times I showed up at the pie shop. I couldn't decide if she was truly busy or avoiding me.

Then her less than enthusiastic reception that morning caused doubt to take root in my heart. Perhaps I had moved too fast and ended up pushing her away instead. She had only lost her husband four months ago. I had close to a year to heal from the loss of Rose.

As I lifted a crate of kitchenware, I shook my head. I set it in the wagon, where James instructed, before I returned to the house for the next one.

"Awfully nice of you to help, Zayne," Boone said as he took the next crate in the stack.

"No trouble."

"I'm sure Violet appreciates it. Jaclyn tells me you've been spending more time with her."

The conversation sounded more like a big brother's warning than friendly banter. I held back a sigh.

"A lot of suitors have hurt her."

"Anyone besides Andrew Ward and Cooper James?" I wondered if there were any secrets Violet had not shared.

"So, she's told you about them."

"Yes."

After Boone set the crate in the wagon, he stood in front of me and crossed his arms. I was a tall man, but he stood a few inches taller than me. His shoulders made mine look puny. His eyes clouded when he continued.

"It was one thing for you to play pranks on her in school. But if you toy with her heart..." Boone uncrossed his arms and cracked his knuckles. "You'll deal with me. And him." He jerked his head toward Deacon. "And them." He nodded toward his other brothers and Grady.

"And Papa may find his way to your home. Don't let his age fool you. He's still a crack shot."

My throat constricted even though I had no intention of hurting Violet.

Then Boone laughed and slapped my shoulder. I couldn't decide if he was joking or not, so I flashed him a tight smile. As he headed back into the house, I started breathing again.

When I entered the house, I glanced at Violet. She sat drumming her fingers on the kitchen table. She looked at me and mouthed the words that she was sorry. I gave her a wink and then grabbed the next crate in the stack.

Once we loaded the wagon, I hopped on a stack of crates in the back with Sam, Deacon, Boone, and Grady. James drove the wagon with Violet on the seat next to him. Boone continued to eye me warily.

When we arrived at James's house, I helped unload. Boone

and I carried the heavy wardrobe upstairs to her new room. It was smaller than I expected, and I wondered if it had been a child's room. Pink curtains brightened the space. The large piece of furniture barely fit against the opposite wall.

After Boone and I set it down, I lingered and asked Violet if she wanted to talk about what was bothering her. When she refused to talk to me, I pressed her.

"Is this related to the other night?"

"No."

When she looked away, it did not convince me. In fact, the more she avoided me, the more I thought it had everything to do with me kissing her or my declaration of love. I could think of no other reason she acted so disengaged.

"Please don't push me away."

"Zayne, please leave me be."

The words that followed bounced off my ears. After all the problems I helped her with, she still didn't trust me. I thought I had earned it by then. I grumbled something and stalked out of her room.

As we finished, she finally came downstairs. Even though she thanked each of us, her gratitude toward me felt stilted. My heart broke as I kissed her cheek.

Then I turned and walked up the street toward my home. I stuffed my hands in my pockets and set a brisk pace. She asked me to kiss her a second time last week. I thought that meant she loved me or was starting to. Yet, her attitude toward me that day felt like rejection.

The next day, she did not attend church. Keri said she wasn't feeling well. That news failed to ease my fears as it reminded me of the number of Sundays Rose missed and how many times heartbreak followed it.

At Sunday supper, Mama commented on my mood.

"Why are you out of sorts?"

I sighed heavily. "I'm not sure, but I think I upset Violet. She won't talk to me."

Mama smiled sympathetically. "Remember that grief does not follow any sort of predictable path. The last week must have been hard, leaving the home she shared with her husband and sorting through his things."

I nodded and poked at my meal with my fork.

When supper was over, I retreated to my room and rocked Eleanor in my arms. Then I laid her in her crib. Her birthday was coming up soon. The thought brought mixed emotions. Happiness that she was healthy. Sadness because her birthday was the same as Rose's death. I hoped in time the memory would fade.

When I returned to the rocking chair with empty arms, I stared out the window. I debated whether I should walk over to James's house to see if Violet would speak with me. I missed her, and I desperately wanted to clear up whatever misunderstanding stood between us.

No. She asked me to leave her alone.

I stood and made my way downstairs. I picked up the phone and called Keri Colter.

"Good afternoon," I said. "Is she feeling any better?"

"She is. She is in the playroom with Will. Would you like to talk to her?"

"No. I don't want to disturb her time with him. Let her know I asked after her."

She agreed, and I ended the call.

———

Even though I wanted to, I didn't go to the pie shop for a week. I also talked myself out of stopping by Violet's house for a walk. The longer I went without seeing her, the more miserable I was. I thought for certain she would eventually reach out to me if she missed me.

I shook off my melancholy and sat down at my desk in the freight office. After picking up the earpiece, I asked the operator to call Henry in Phoenix.

"Hello?"

"Morning, Henry."

"Zayne! How are things in Prescott?"

"Good. Look, I was calling to see what you think about me using the title Chief Operating Officer? I need a little more clout behind my name when I'm negotiating with the railways. Just saying I'm a partner doesn't seem to get me anywhere."

"Hmm. That makes sense to me. But Martin might not be happy."

"Perhaps we should make him the President & CEO? You could be the Chief Logistics Officer."

"You know I manage the financial side, so what about Chief Financial Officer for me?"

"Yeah, that works for me."

"Alright. Let me talk to Martin and see what he says."

We both hung up. A half hour later, he rang me back.

"Martin likes your idea but thinks your title should be Chief Logistics Officer. The railroads will associate your position with logistics and know you can negotiate rates, handle claims, and billing."

"Wait, so you want me to pick up billing?"

"Yes. You can hire someone up there to manage client billing for all locations. I'm going to take over accounts payable and receivables. So, I'll need you to circulate official rate sheets within the entire company."

"Alright."

"I'll send an interoffice memo with the details."

As I put the earpiece back on the receiver, I sighed. I was not prepared to take over client billing.

As I raked a hand through my hair, I stood and crossed the main office area to Al's office. I brought him up to speed with changes.

"I remember interviewing a young lady earlier this year who had experience with billing. I really liked her background, but we didn't have a position that fit."

He opened the filing cabinet and pulled out a file. "Ah, here it is. Naomi Fisk."

After I took the file from his hands, I scanned her resume. "Oh, she has several years' experience. Do you know if she accepted a position somewhere else?"

"I don't. Even if she did, she might be interested if it was not her ideal job."

Once back at my desk, I asked the operator to ring her home. When there was no answer, I assumed she was at another job. So, I set it aside for the evening.

Early in the afternoon, I headed over to the Santa Fe, Prescott, & Phoenix Railway offices for a meeting with Daniel Parker, the Vice President of Transportation. I entered the large two-story building at the depot. Martin told me they moved into the new offices last year. Even though he had warned me it was ostentatious, I was unprepared for it.

The lobby area glittered with polished marble and brass fixtures. The transom ceiling of the main lobby towered high above my head. There was a balcony overlooking the main lobby, lined with dark wood spindles. My shoes clicked as I walked across the marble.

I gave the receptionist my name and asked for Mr. Parker. "Zayne?"

I turned at the sound of my name. "James."

Then I extended my hand in greeting to Violet's brother.

"What brings you by?" he asked.

I told him about my meeting.

"Let me escort you up to Daniel's office."

As I followed James up a large curved, dark wood staircase, he continued talking. "I'm surprised you haven't been by to see Violet lately."

I cleared my throat. "It just seems like she wanted some space."

"She has seemed melancholy, but I think she would appreciate a visit from you."

They had decorated the hallway walls with a gold fleur-de-lis pattern on a robin's egg blue background. Dark wood wainscoting covered the bottom third of the wall.

"Here we are," he said as he stopped in front of an open door.

"Daniel," James said, "I ran into Zayne in the lobby and brought him up. I hope you don't mind."

"Not at all. A pleasure to meet you, Zayne," Daniel said as he shook my hand.

"Hope we'll see you at the house soon," James said before he left and closed the door behind him.

"Oh, I didn't realize you were friends with the Colters," Daniel commented as he rounded to the other side of his desk.

"I'm courting his sister."

Daniel failed to mask his surprise at first. Then he shuffled some papers as he smiled.

"You're here to talk about rates?"

"Yes."

We spent the next hour reviewing the list of rates for all the destinations on the SFP&P and their Prescott & Eastern Railway branch line. I negotiated a volume discount for our offices in Phoenix, Prescott, and the other towns along the branch line.

As I was getting ready to leave, Daniel mentioned an unusual connection with Violet. "I always felt sorry for her, ever since my sister Catherine ended up marrying Andrew Ward. The two of them treated her rather unfairly."

"Did you know Violet?"

"She worked in the cafeteria for a few years. She was always friendly with all the staff. It did not surprise me to hear she opened a pie shop. She bakes the best pie."

I laughed. "I can attest to that."

"Anyway, please tell her she has been in my wife and my prayers."

"Will do."

He escorted me to the lobby and shook my hand before I left.

As I walked back to my office, I debated about stopping by the pie shop. I decided not to and surprise her at home that evening instead.

When I returned to the office, I rang Ms. Naomi Fisk again. That time, she answered.

"Hello?"

"Ms. Fisk? This is Zayne Harrison, the Chief Logistics Officer for J.W. Harrison & Co."

"Yes?"

"You spoke with our general manager, Albert Sharpe, a few months ago."

"Oh, yes. I remember now."

"We have a new position I would like to discuss with you. Would you be able to stop by our office tomorrow?"

"Um. I took a position already."

"Please stop by and let me tell you about the opportunity. I think it suits your background."

She finally agreed, and we set up a time. I penciled it in my calendar as I wished her a good evening.

Then I called Keri Colter to invite myself to dinner. I told her about my conversation with James, and she assured me I was welcome to come for dinner at six.

After I went home to check on Eleanor and make sure Mama agreed to watch her, I headed over to the Colter's home. I hoped Violet would be happy to see me. I missed her so very much.

CHAPTER 19

VIOLET

As I headed home for the day, I rubbed my back. In my sixth month, my condition became difficult to conceal. I sighed as I wiped my hand across my forehead. The air was thick with humidity. I glanced at the sky and hoped the rainfall would wait until I arrived home.

When the wind picked up, a few strands of my hair stuck to my face, so I hooked them behind my ear.

Splat. Plop. Several fat raindrops landed on my head at the halfway mark on my route home. The raindrops picked up momentum, and I ducked under the awning of a building.

The air cooled, and I breathed deeply of the sweet smell of rain.

"In other parts of the country, the rain doesn't smell as nice."

I remembered Forest's words to me. He grew up near Chicago.

"In fact, back home, the rain made the stench of the city worse."

As we sat under the cover of our porch, he took a deep breath.

"I once asked a botanist friend of mine why our rain smells so sweet."

"Oh?"

Forest laughed. "He said there is this bush in the desert called a creosote. It secretes oil right before the rain comes. That's what we smell. The oil from the creosote bush."

I took another deep breath of the creosote-scented air. Because I was born in the Arizona Territory and never traveled beyond Prescott, it had always been the smell of rain for me.

The rain poured from the sky and lightning flashed overhead. A young woman darted across the street and took shelter next to me. She laughed as she patted her blond hair.

"That caught me by surprise. Looks like you made it before it came down too hard."

Something looked familiar about her, like I had seen her before. Perhaps at church? No. Or a store? I shook my head when I couldn't place it.

"Only just."

A motorized carriage pulled to a stop next to us. The driver said my name.

"Yes?"

"My name is Mr. Wilson. Mr. Colter asked me to find you and drive you home."

I raised an eyebrow, as his name was unfamiliar to me.

"I am Mr. Murphy's driver."

"Thank you," I said as I walked under the shelter of his umbrella to the automobile.

Mr. Wilson closed the door behind me before he took the driver's seat again. We only made it two blocks before I spotted a familiar man. I smiled and my heart flipped.

"That's Zayne. Can you stop for him?"

"Certainly."

Mr. Wilson pulled the vehicle to a stop as I tapped on the window. I grinned as Zayne lifted his head. He smiled and reached for the handle. Then he slid into the front seat next to Mr. Wilson.

"Thank you for stopping," he said. "I knew I should have brought my umbrella."

After the two men introduced themselves, I asked, "Where are you headed?"

"To the flower shop, then on to your house."

"Oh?"

"Yes, Keri invited me to come for supper. She said it's been far too long since I've been by. We can forgo the flower shop, given the weather."

Mr. Wilson raised an eyebrow but said nothing. I was certain he noticed my condition and thought our conversation odd. No matter.

"Sorry to drip water all over your automobile," Zayne said.

"I will clean it up before Mr. Murphy ever knows."

When the driver stopped in front of James's house, James stood waiting on his porch with an umbrella. He held the automobile door open for me.

"I can't thank you enough, Mr. Wilson," James said, and handed the man a few bills. "And thank Frank for me."

Mr. Wilson nodded once as Zayne exited and dashed out into the rain and onto the safety of the porch. James offered his arm to me and the cover of the umbrella. When we were on the porch, he shook the water off the umbrella. Then he set it in the entryway.

"I see the rain caught you," he said to Zayne.

"Unfortunately, yes."

James asked him to wait in the entryway, so I waited with him.

"You said Keri invited you?" I asked, so glad to see him again. Relieved even. Especially since I'd been so rude to him on the day he had helped me move.

"Yes. I hope that is alright with you." He angled his head and glanced out of the corner of his eye.

I stretched up to kiss his cheek. Then I laughed. "You are

drenched."

James's housekeeper appeared with some towels and a change of clothes for Zayne. Then she escorted him to the first-floor powder room.

As I entered the dining room, the cook had just finished setting out the meal. I took my seat, and we waited for Zayne. When he appeared, he wore one of James's suits and his hair was sticking every which way.

"Come here," I said.

Once he sat next to me, I smoothed out his hair.

"That's better."

Following the blessing, the conversation flowed.

"Did Daniel settle everything to your satisfaction?" James asked.

"Yes, of course," Zayne replied. "Violet, he asked me to let you know that he and his wife have been praying for you."

"Daniel?"

"Parker," James said.

When I recognized the name, I held back a frown. I held no ill feelings towards him or his wife. Only his sister.

As James and Keri spoke softly to each other for a few minutes, Zayne angled toward me.

"Sorry I haven't been by. I thought you wanted some space."

"When you came by the pie shop, I was truly busy. I'm sorry you thought I was avoiding you."

"How are you feeling?"

"Exhausted most days. I can hardly wait to get these shoes off."

He winked conspiratorially. "You should visit the powder room and take them off then."

My cheeks heated. "It can wait until after supper."

After a minute, I whispered, "I missed you."

The last of the tension between us melted away as he smiled. Then he ate a bite of his meal.

Tate, James's twelve-year-old, said, "I thought Grandpa didn't like the Harrisons."

My eyes rounded, and Zayne choked.

"That is news to me," Keri said. "I'm certain Papa was close friends with Zayne's papa."

"He was," Zayne said.

"Not Grandpa Glassman. Grandpa Colter," Tate clarified.

I looked at James. He shook his head and shrugged.

"Don't be silly," Keri said. "Grandpa Colter likes every-one."

I wondered where Tate got such a notion.

Their nine-year-old daughter, Geneva, quickly changed the subject to her excitement over the start of school the next week. Madeline, the seven-year-old, agreed.

"Will Patrick start school this year?" I asked.

"He doesn't turn five until October, so I'm uncertain," Keri said.

"He's too restless. We should wait until next year," James said. "Maybe he'll settle down and have a better experience."

Once supper finished, the children, including Will, ran upstairs to play. James showed Zayne to his study for an after-dinner drink while Keri invited me to the parlor. After a quick trip upstairs to remove my shoes and braid my hair, I returned downstairs.

Keri slid a footstool in front of the couch.

"Bless you." I sat and propped my stocking-clad feet on the stool. "If Zayne wasn't here, I would probably soak my feet."

"I doubt he would mind," she teased.

"James would think me scandalous."

"It was good to see you smiling when you came home."

"I'm glad you invited Zayne. It made me realize I should have done so already."

A few minutes later, Zayne and James joined us. After Zayne sat next to me and settled his arm around my shoulders, I leaned into his side and rested my head on his shoulder. I missed him so much and regretted letting my sorrow over the mystery woman affect my relationship with him.

The rest of the evening flew by as he told me about his work at the freight office. His eyes lit with excitement as he talked. After I caught him up on the news about me and Will, I told him about the pie shop.

"You should stop by on Wednesday for a late lunch," I suggested. "I'm trying out a new pot pie recipe."

"But you already have chicken and beef."

I winked at him. "You must stop by to see what I have up my sleeve."

He took my hand and examined my arm. "I don't think a pot pie will fit in your sleeve."

All four of us laughed. It made me happy to smile and laugh with him again.

When the nanny appeared at seven-thirty to let me know Will was ready for his bed-time story, I invited Zayne to join me. After we climbed the stairs, I rubbed my low back while I walked down the hall.

"Are you sure you're feeling alright?"

"Yes. Why do you ask?"

"You've been rubbing your back. A lot." He took my hand as we stood outside of Will's room. "It's just that…"

"Rose did that too."

He blinked rapidly and nodded.

"I think most women carrying a child do so. It doesn't mean something is wrong."

"I don't want to lose you, Violet."

My breath caught at the intensity in his eyes.

The nanny cleared her throat, breaking the moment. She held the door open. As my cheeks warmed, I followed her into the room.

"Zay!" Will greeted him. "Read story?"

"Absolutely, little man."

As he sat on the edge of the bed, I handed him one of Will's story books. Then I walked around to the other side and sat next to Will. I propped my feet up and listened to Zayne's very animated storytelling.

I loved how his expressions changed to match the mood of the story. Will giggled at Zayne's exaggerated animation. He was so good with my son. My heart tugged. He would be a wonderful father to Will. Though I wished Forest could be there to raise our son, Zayne was more than up to the challenge.

"Again!" Will demanded.

Zayne looked at me. I nodded. By the time he made it halfway through the story, Will fell asleep. I brushed his hair back from his face. Then Zayne leaned forward and kissed his forehead.

"Good night, little man."

After Zayne stood, I tried to get up but felt like Will's bed swallowed me whole. Zayne held out his hands and helped me to my feet.

"I should go," he whispered once we stood in the hallway. "I want to make it home before Eleanor falls asleep."

I escorted him downstairs and led him to the entryway.

"Let James know I'll return his clothes soon."

I nodded.

Then he pulled me into his safe arms. As he lowered his head, I slid my hands behind his neck. His lips met mine with a gentle, sweet kiss. Too soon, he reluctantly ended the kiss but kept his hands at my waist.

"Eleanor's birthday is on Friday." His voice caught and his eyes reddened. "Sorry. I didn't expect…"

"It must be hard. To celebrate her birth must feel strange, as it was when her mother passed."

As tears pooled in his eyes, he pinched the bridge of his nose. I stretched up to kiss him softly, offering my comfort. When I ended the kiss, he gave me a half smile.

"Can you and Will join us on Friday?"

"Of course."

He released his hold on me and turned toward the door.

"Good night, Violet."

"Good night."

I closed the door behind him. Then I went up to my room. I changed into a nightgown and sat on my bed.

When I reached for my Bible, the photograph of Forest's mystery woman fell into my lap. I glared at the woman.

"Who are you? How did you know Forest?"

The photograph failed to answer, so I stuffed it in the front cover before I flipped to the Psalms. I found a few that soothed the hurt in my heart.

CHAPTER 20

ZAYNE

On Wednesday morning, Naomi Fisk arrived a few minutes early. I escorted her to my office but left the door open. She wore a plain white blouse and a dark brown skirt. She had pulled her blond hair into a twist at the base of her neck. Her brown eyes lit as she smiled.

"It looks like you've expanded since I was here last."

I offered her a chair across from my desk. Then I took a seat.

"Yes, I want to discuss it with you. Thank you for coming by."

"Of course."

"I'm not sure how much Al told you about our company. My late father started the company over thirty years ago. We have offices in Tucson, Phoenix, Prescott, and nearly every town in the territory."

She nodded.

"With the number of locations we have, we believe certain operations make more sense at a company level versus handling them at each location. One of those operations is client billing."

"I see."

"When I mentioned a new billing department, Al suggested I contact you." I glanced down at the copy of her resume. "Your experience matches what we need."

She explained her background in more detail. Then we discussed how she might organize a billing department.

"At first, you would be the only employee in the department. Once we're organized, we'll hire more people. You would report directly to me."

"It sounds like a wonderful position."

"How did you decide to live in Prescott?"

She glanced away. "I fell on hard times. My brother suggested that a friend in the area might help me get on my feet."

Naomi turned her gaze back to me. "Unfortunately, I could not locate that friend. I was, however, able to secure a position at a shop in town to provide the income I needed."

"Tell me I have convinced you this position would be more in line with your talents."

"I would love to be a part of J.W. Harrison & Co."

I smiled. "Excellent."

We worked out the details about her salary and start date. Then I escorted her to the front office.

"A pleasure to meet you, Ms. Fisk."

"And you, Mr. Harrison."

When she left, my stomach growled. I glanced at the clock on the wall. Only half-past twelve. Too early to visit the pie shop. So, I worked on some paperwork in my office until a quarter after one. Then I donned my hat and headed over to see Violet.

When I arrived, Zola led me to the table in the kitchen.

"Right on time," Violet said as she rubbed her low back.

I frowned. "How are you feeling?"

"You worry too much, Zayne," she said as she squeezed my hand.

That didn't keep me from worrying. After everything I went through with Rose, of course, I was acting over-protective.

"Have a seat."

I sat as she set a plate in front of me.

"Enjoy."

"Aren't you having some?" I asked.

"I will. I want to hear what you think first."

I eyed her warily. "I'm not sure I trust you."

She laughed and turned back toward the stove. After she dished up one for herself on a plate, she sat across from me.

"Go ahead."

I poked the bottom of the pie with a spoon. A creamy soup oozed from the opening. The aroma of bacon, cheese, and chives wafted up.

"Smells delicious." I ate a bite. "Potato soup?"

"With?"

"Bacon, cheese, and chives."

"And?"

I shook my head.

"It was a trick question."

I smiled. "You got me."

I took another bite of the savory meal. "It's very good. The bacon adds just the right amount of saltiness."

"I'm glad you like it."

After she ate a few bites, she placed a hand on her extend-ed belly. "Oof."

"She's been very active today."

I quirked an eyebrow. "She?"

"I'm guessing. Come here."

When I leaned forward, Violet placed my hand on her belly. I felt it and grinned.

"She's kicking."

"Oh, I feel it."

She laughed. "It's the strangest feeling. She is more active than Will."

"Hard to believe. Especially how squirmy he is now."

"He was the most pleasant baby. It's once he joined the world that he became so rambunctious."

I leaned back in my chair and finished my pot pie.

"Not going to eat more?"

She shifted in her chair and frowned. "I will when she settles down."

"You should ask James to drive you to and from work now."

"I'll consider it."

"I just don't want—"

"I know." She reached across the table and squeezed my hand. "Don't worry."

I swallowed back my fear of losing her. Then I stood and kissed her cheek before I returned to work. I really hoped she was not overdoing things.

———

On Friday, I rented a carriage and picked up Will from James's house before I picked up Violet from the pie shop.

"This is a pleasant surprise." She smiled as I helped her into the carriage.

She placed her hand on her abdomen.

"It kicks," Will said.

"Yes." She placed his hand on it.

Will giggled.

"Are you feeling up to this?" I asked.

"Yes. I would have said so."

"Alright. We'll have people in and out. My sisters wanted

to stop by on Eleanor's birthday. I reminded them we cannot all fit in the house."

Violet held my free hand. "That will be nice."

When we arrived, I set the brake and tied the reins to the post in front of the house. I helped Violet down. Then I took Will's hand and led them into the house.

Miss Harmony took Will to the side of the parlor where my nieces and nephews played.

"I guess they showed up at the same time."

I offered Violet a place on the couch. As Mama handed Eleanor to Pearl, I kissed my daughter. Then I greeted each of my sisters.

"Papa!"

My heart nearly stopped. "Did she just call me—"

"Papa, yes." Mama smiled. "She did."

My eyes burned, and I held out my arms for my baby girl. "Yes, Ella. I'm your Papa."

"Papa!" She smiled.

After that, it took some time before my sisters convinced me to let them hold her. I sat next to Violet and bounced Eleanor on my knee.

"I heard that," Violet said. "Was that the first time she's called you Papa?"

"Yes." I beamed.

"What a wonderful birthday gift."

Mama announced that supper was ready. My sisters fixed plates for their children. Then I placed Eleanor in her highchair next to me. I set a plate of small pieces of meat and potatoes in front of her. She stuffed them in her mouth. Then she threw a few pieces. I didn't mind. She called me Papa.

My sisters asked Violet lots of questions while we ate. I warned them to let her eat since she had a rowdy baby to support.

"You're carrying like he's a boy," Cora said.

"Oh?" Violet asked.

"Most definitely a boy," Beulah said.

"I agree," Wilma said.

"I don't know," Mabel said. "I could never tell a difference."

"I'm sure it's a boy," Alice said.

Victoria laughed. "It's impossible to know for sure. Remember when I carried Albert?"

Mama nodded. "Yes. We thought he would be a girl."

I laughed. "I'm going to tease him about that at work."

"My point is," Victoria said, "that you don't know until they arrive. Anything before that is a lucky guess."

Mama stood and brought in a piece of cake for Eleanor. Then we all sang Happy Birthday. I laughed as Ella squeezed the cake through her fingers a few times before she brought it up to her mouth. When she did, her eyes rounded, and she licked the smashed cake from her fingers.

"Zayne," Pearl whispered to me.

She nodded to the doorway where Violet stood gripping the door jamb with white knuckles.

I stood and rushed to her side. "Vi?"

"Oh, I'm sorry. I didn't want to—" She groaned and grabbed her abdomen.

"Here." I led her to the closest chair in the parlor.

The memories from a year ago washed over me. Rose gripping the doorway. Holding her stomach. Tears streamed down her face. She collapsed. I had to leave her alone to fetch the doctor.

Three of my sisters gathered around. They started asking Violet several questions until they determined she had some indigestion. I blew out a loud breath.

Mama placed a hand on my shoulder as she whispered,

"She'll be fine. I will have Jedediah take her home."

"No, I'll go."

I kissed Eleanor goodbye, and she rewarded me with another, "Papa."

Then I helped Violet to the carriage before I returned to the house to get Will. I carried him even though he squirmed. He settled when he sat between me and Violet.

"I'm so sorry to ruin Eleanor's birthday."

"You didn't ruin it."

"I—" She groaned again.

"Should I take you to the doctor?"

"I want you to breathe. You're very pale, Zayne, and you are scaring my son."

I took a deep breath and let it out slowly.

"I will be fine. Like your sisters said, it's just something not sitting well on my stomach."

By the time we reached James's house, she seemed much improved. Will ran up the stairs into the house, leaving the door open. I helped Violet down from the carriage and into the house.

"Thank you for driving me. I will talk to James about getting me a driver for work."

"Please rest tomorrow. I think you are pushing yourself too hard."

She smiled, but her eyes clouded. "I'm fine."

Then she kissed my cheek and bid me farewell.

As I dropped off the carriage and walked home, I worried the entire way. After finally being free to love Violet, I could not deal with possibly losing her.

CHAPTER 21

VIOLET

Katie and Zola managed the pie shop without me for a few days. I slept late and read a book in the parlor. To my delight, Zayne stopped by on Saturday afternoon with Eleanor.

"Miss me?" he asked as he entered the parlor.

As I pushed the footstool aside, he said, "Don't get up."

Then he walked over to me and placed a kiss on my cheek. I smiled when he sat next to me on the couch.

"How are you feeling?"

"Much better. Seems I needed a little extra sleep."

When I set my book aside, he placed his arm around me.

"Mmm. I missed you," I said as I leaned into his side.

"I missed you too."

He cleared his throat. "I thought, if you're feeling up to it, you could join me for Sunday supper. Just you and me tomorrow."

"Sounds nice."

We talked about his work for a bit. Then he told me he checked for me every day at the pie shop.

"I was glad to hear you took some time off. I've been worried about you."

I patted my hand on his leg. "You need to stop worrying.

I have three months left."

When he rested his head against the top of mine, I continued.

"I understand what you went through with Rose is on your mind. I'm not Rose. And every pregnancy is different. Remember, God is in control of it all."

As he ran his fingers along my arm, he whispered, "I don't want to lose you, Violet. I love you. I want us to have many wonderful years together."

"I… I just need to focus on having this baby and getting settled with a newborn. It will take time before I am ready to marry."

He angled to look into my eyes. "But you will consider it?"

I sighed. "Yes. This baby will consume my life soon. I don't want to push you away, but you may feel like that is happening."

His eyes searched mine for several seconds as he trailed his fingers along the side of my neck. A thrilling shiver ran through my body at his touch.

"Think about how you coped after Eleanor was born."

Slowly, he nodded. "I think I understand."

"A baby takes over one's time. For months on end. Because we aren't married, you may not see much of me."

"We could change that."

I searched his eyes. "We don't know each other very well. We're both trying to parent our children. I'm expecting another child. It's terrible timing for talk of a wedding, much less actually doing it."

He leaned forward and brushed his lips across mine. My stomach fluttered, and I wanted a longer kiss but I leaned away.

"Please be patient, Zayne."

When his shoulders slumped, I realized how much he loved me. I loved him too. Marrying him with a baby on the way would be foolish, even though I wanted his help with my baby.

"I understand," he said at length. "You'll still come tomorrow?"

I nodded as he stood. He gave me a half smile before he collected his daughter and left.

For several minutes, I stared after him, wondering if I made the right decision.

―――――

ZAYNE

If she had not been pregnant, Violet would have married me soon. Instead, she tried to prepare me that such a decision was months away. I wondered if it was much longer than I thought.

After Eleanor's birth, it took me nearly six months before I responded to my family's offer of help. They persuaded me to move back to Prescott three months later. Once Violet gave birth, it'd be at least six months before she'd be ready for a genuine relationship with me. I shuffled my feet as I walked back toward home while pushing Eleanor's carriage in front of me.

A year. That was the most realistic time frame. I would wait for her. As long as it took, I would wait.

The next day, following church, Mama and Jedediah headed over to Cora's home for Sunday supper. Mama gave me and Violet some time alone. James paid for a carriage from church to my house. After the driver dropped us off, he returned to church for James's family. I steadied Violet as we walked up the porch stairs together. The house seemed quiet as we entered. Harmony already put Eleanor down for a nap, and Violet had sent Will home with Keri. It was truly the two of us.

When I held a chair for her at the dining table, she sighed as she sat down. "It's so peaceful here."

Miss Vera set out a platter of roast chicken, a bowl of mashed potatoes, gravy, and some roasted carrots. The food smelled amazing. Then she disappeared and brought back a pitcher of iced tea.

She said to let her know if we needed anything else. Before I prayed for the meal, I thanked her. Once the blessing finished, Violet smiled at me.

"This is very nice."

My heart longed to make a life with her. I thought about begging her to marry me so I could care for her. I wanted to. But I understood the wisdom in her request to be patient.

As we ate, I told her stories from my childhood.

"Growing up in a huge family was normal for me," I said. "Always noisy. Someone picking on someone else. Games and play time. Vying for Papa and Mama's attention. Though that wasn't necessary. They both did their best to devote time to each of us. I don't know how they did it."

"With five older brothers, there always seemed to be noise at my home, too. Though, when I was twelve, they started marrying off and having children of their own. It was strange moving into the smaller ranch house with only Mama and Papa. So quiet."

"I know what you mean. My brothers and sisters started marrying and moving out, too. Two or three people set off each year to find their own life."

She ate a few bites before saying it was the natural way of

things. I allowed the conversation to wane for a few minutes while I concentrated on eating.

"It seemed odd to come back as an adult with my own child. I'm living in the same room that I used to share with several brothers. Now it's me and Eleanor."

"Will you move her to her own room soon?"

"I think so. It's probably time."

I turned my gaze to Violet. Her lovely eyes sparkled with life. Light pink colored her cheeks as she reached out for my hand.

"The first one is hard. You want them to stay small forever. Before you know it, they've outgrown their crib and start talking back."

I snorted. "Do you have a crib for your little one?"

She nodded. "I brought it when I moved. I should ask James to pull it out of the shed soon."

"Will you put it in your room? Is there space?"

She sighed. "You're right, the room is small. But I don't want my baby with the nanny."

The silence stretched for a minute before I spoke again.

"I think Mama is going to give the house to me."

"This vast house, for just you and Eleanor?"

"And Miss Harmony and Miss Vera. I think Mama feels like she's not much help. But she is. I feel better just knowing she's here."

Violet pushed her empty plate away. "Perhaps she really longs for some privacy with her husband."

My face heated at the thought. "Maybe."

I wondered if there was more to it. Perhaps Mama knew it was just a matter of time before I married again.

I cleared my throat. "Shall we retire to the parlor?"

Violet stood slowly. I studied her carefully, noticing every change in her expression. Without realizing it, I watched for signs of pain.

With Rose, she miscarried long before this stage of her pregnancy. Eleanor was the only child carried to term.

"Zayne," Violet whispered my name. "I know it's hard for you. Please don't worry."

I let out a loud breath as I walked next to her into the parlor. She sat on the couch and lifted her feet as I scooted the footstool close. Then I sat beside her.

"Where do we go from here? I mean, if marriage isn't an option for a year…"

"A year?" she asked. "I suppose you're right. It is the most realistic time frame."

As I wrapped my arm around her shoulders, I let out a slow breath. "I guess we court for a year then."

I turned to face her. Then I placed my hand on her chin and lowered my lips to hers. I kissed her softly for a breath before I leaned back.

"As long as you feel up to it," I said, "I'd like to dine together often. Is twice a week and Sundays good?"

"I'd like that. I'm sure Keri and James won't mind."

"We could eat here sometimes if you still feel like coming over here."

"I will look forward to it," she whispered.

Even though I longed for her to be my wife, I resolved to be patient. Compared to a lifetime, a year seemed insignificant.

CHAPTER 22

September 11, 1906

VIOLET

At seven months, I felt large and round. I didn't remember what my feet looked like. As I leaned down to pull some pies out of the oven, I felt light-headed.

"Here, let me," Zola said as she grabbed the pie with a towel. "You should let me help more."

As I blotted my forehead with my handkerchief, I sighed. No matter what I did, my body felt like fire.

"Why don't you sit in a chair outside? I put a little table out there. I'll bring you water in just a minute."

"Alright."

I waddled to the open door and sat on the chair while I fanned my face.

"Here," Zola said as she handed me water.

As I sipped the water, I prayed for a cool breeze. I closed my eyes and rested my head against the building. There were two more months left. I sighed.

When I opened my eyes, I spotted Zayne near the docks. His long legs and easy gait brought a smile to my face. A blond woman stood talking to him. Her back was to me.

Once he spotted me, he waved. The woman turned and my stomach clenched. She looked familiar, but at that distance, I couldn't place her.

"Oof." I clutched my abdomen and gritted my teeth. Out of the corner of my eye, I noticed Zayne ran toward me.

"Violet, are you alright?"

The fear in his voice warmed my heart. I wished he would not worry so much, but I completely understood it, especially after what he went through with his wife.

"Afternoon," I said as I tried to catch my breath. I didn't remember feeling so terrible when I was pregnant with Will.

When his brow furrowed, I gave him a wan smile.

"Who is." I took a deep breath. "The woman?"

The blond went about her business with a worker at the dock.

"That's Naomi Fisk. I told you about her, right?"

I nodded.

"She's the client billing manager. I was introducing her to some employees at the railway."

"Eat yet?" I asked as my breathing returned to normal.

"No. I was hoping to stop by if you can join me." His soft blue-gray eyes still held a hint of concern.

When I stood, I bumped into my glass of water. It fell over the edge of the table and shattered. Tears sprang to my eyes.

"It's alright. I'll sweep it up," Zayne said as he helped me the rest of the way to my feet. Then he led me to the table inside.

Zola must have heard, because she had a broom in hand. She stared intently at Zayne. "Please convince her to go home. She needs to rest."

"I don't need to rest." My tears were gone and anger replaced it. I remembered this from carrying Will. Emotions that made no sense. Poor Forest went through it right along with me. If Zayne stuck with me through this, he could make it through anything.

"She's right," he said. "Let me send for a carriage or call James to have you driven home."

"I'm. Fine." Breathless again. Ugh.

Katie brought Zayne some coffee and a beef pot pie. When she raised an eyebrow, I nodded. She brought me the same. As soon as Zayne finished sweetening his coffee, Naomi entered.

"There you are," she said.

"Ms. Fisk, meet my sweetheart, Violet Gamble."

I gave her a weak smile. "Would you care for a late lunch?"

She shook her head. "I ate a sandwich earlier."

Her eyes narrowed for a moment. "Have we met before?"

I looked her over. Then I realized where I had seen her. "The rain."

"Ah, yes. That's right. We took shelter under the same awning. An automobile picked you up."

I smiled. "Yes, that's right. It's a pleasure to meet you."

Suddenly, my heart sank to the pit of my stomach. I recognized her from somewhere else too.

"Were you born in 1881?" I asked.

Naomi frowned. "How did you—"

Anger boiled to the surface. "It's you. You're the woman."

I reached into my apron pocket and slapped the picture of her down on the table.

Naomi's hand shook as she reached for the picture. "How did you get this?"

I snorted. "So you didn't recognize my name. Gamble. *Mrs.* Forest Gamble."

Slowly, she shook her head. When she turned the picture over, her frown deepened. "This is my address. Where did you get this?"

"Violet, what is going on?" Zayne asked.

Katie and Zola scurried from the kitchen during the discussion. Sweat beaded on my forehead and I wiped my arm across it.

"It was in Forest's Bible. How did you know my late husband?"

The woman had a strange connection with my husband. Now she worked for my new beau. Seemed too odd to be a coincidence.

Zayne reached for the picture. "This was in Forest's Bible?"

I glared at him.

Naomi slid into a chair. Her lips parted several times, but no sound came.

"Spit it out," I demanded. "How did you know Forest?"

"I... I didn't. This..."

She turned the picture over. "This is the photograph I sent to my half-brother down in Mexico."

My head hurt. Her words made no sense. "What does your half-brother have to do with anything?"

"This is his. Cooper James. I sent it to him."

The name landed on my heart like a bullet. I coughed as bile rose in the back of my throat. Cooper. Forest. Zayne.

"Did I wrong you in my life that you would come after all the men I loved?"

Zayne reached for my hand. "Violet, you look pale. Calm down."

"Calm down?" I shrieked.

"She knows Cooper—my fiancé that disappeared without a trace. And her photo was in Forest's Bible. Now she works for you. That seems suspicious to me."

"I contacted Naomi. She had interviewed with Al early this year and we didn't have a position for her then. When I moved here and started the centralized billing, Al suggested her resume."

Zayne turned my face to look at him. "She could not have known I would call her or that I was in any way connected with you."

I shook my head. "It makes no sense."

My pulse raced, and the room felt as warm as a furnace. I blotted my face with my apron.

"I agree," Naomi said. "I moved here because Cooper suggested I look up a Miss Colter. He thought she might have connections to help me find a new job. To start over."

I slammed my palm on the table. "I am Violet Colter-Gamble."

Naomi's brown eyes widened. "You're Miss Colter?"

"I was when Cooper knew me. When did you talk to him?"

"I haven't talked to him in years. We've corresponded by letter. He sent me an address in Mexico where he received letters. I sent him this picture and told him about the… That I needed to move out of Tucson."

Her slender fingers fiddled with the edge of the photograph.

"He sent me a letter saying he'd write to you. Plead for help."

I snorted. Then a sharp pain squeezed my abdomen. Hard. Like contractions.

My eyes widened. My breath left me. I panted, and the room spun.

CHAPTER 23

ZAYNE

As Violet grew paler, I wrapped my arm around her. Suddenly, she went limp.

"Zola, call for an ambulance!" I yelled.

"Naomi, go back to work. We'll talk about this later."

She nodded and left with the photograph.

"Violet. Violet!"

I shook her, but she didn't respond. The ambulance took forever to arrive. My heart hammered against my rib cage. I didn't move. I held onto her, afraid to leave her side.

The men from the ambulance entered through the back door. I relayed as much information about her condition as I could. When they carried her out on the stretcher, I leaped to my feet. I joined her in the back of the wagon.

Within minutes, we arrived at the hospital. A stern nurse greeted me.

"Are you her husband?"

"No. She's my—"

"If you're not family, you can't enter."

"But—"

"If she has family nearby, I suggest you contact them."

I sank into a chair. "Will she be alright?"

The nurse frowned and turned on her heel.

My stomach clenched as tight as my fist. I had to get back there. I had to check on her.

"Zayne?" A soft voice drew my attention.

"Keri. I don't know how she is. Please find out."

Keri nodded. "I called James. He was going to call the family. I'll head back with her so she won't be alone. As soon as I can, I'll update you."

I rested my elbows on my knees and dropped my head into my hands.

Please, Lord, keep Violet safe.

My mind spun over the strange conversation from earlier. Naomi was Cooper's half-sister. Cooper, Violet's fiancé that disappeared. Forest had her picture. I shook my head. None of it made sense, and all of it fractured Violet's heart.

I wanted to run to her side and hold her in my arms. To tell her none of the past mattered. I was here now. She would be safe with me. I would protect her.

Protect her. I was a fool to believe I actually could.

"Zayne." Keri placed a hand on my shoulder.

When I looked up, she took a seat next to me.

"She'll be fine. So will the baby."

I let out a shaky breath.

"The doctor thinks the stress triggered false contractions. He wants her to take it easy for a few weeks. James is coming with an automobile to pick her up. We're going to take her home. I'll call you later, alright?"

I nodded numbly.

"Why don't you head home?"

I stood and stuffed my hands in my pockets. Then I headed back to the office.

When I entered, I headed straight for Naomi's office.

"How is she?"

"Alright. Her brother is taking her home now."

Naomi let out a breath. "I'm so sorry. I do not know how her late husband ended up with my picture."

As I sank into the chair across from her, I frowned. "Don't you?"

She shook her head. "I've been trying to figure it out. Cooper told me he wrote to Violet Colter for her help. He wanted her to help me find a place to live and a job."

To ease my headache, I rubbed my fingers on my temples.

"You don't think Forest intercepted the letter, do you?" she asked.

I sat up straighter. "That's possible. It would explain why he had your picture."

If I were Forest and I received a letter for Violet under her maiden name with a return address from C. James or Cooper James, I'd certainly open it. If he had, perhaps, he investigated it before sharing it with Violet.

"When did you arrive in Prescott?"

"The first week of April."

"April..." Forest died during the month. "I think he must have read the letter from your brother and had not shared it with Violet before he passed. In April."

Naomi's mouth formed a large "O" as she nodded her head. "That makes sense."

The phone rang, cutting through the silence. She answered it. When she started shuffling through papers on her desk, I left.

It was still a little early in the day, but I headed home anyway. When I arrived, I told Mama what happened, and that I expected a call from the Colters later. Then I headed upstairs to find Eleanor and spend time with my sweet daughter.

After supper, Violet called.

"Zayne?"

"Violet." Her name left my voice on a breath.

"I'm alright. I'm home now. Before I head upstairs, I wanted to talk to you."

"You sound tired."

"I am. About that conversation. Can you do me a favor?"

"Anything."

"Can you figure out what happened? I... I want to know. No matter what the truth is. I need to know."

I heard James scold her in the background.

"Alright. I've gotta go. I love you."

My heart warmed. "Love you."

The line went dead.

I breathed deeply and let it out slowly. I sent a brief prayer of gratitude heavenward. She and her baby were fine.

The next morning, I asked Naomi to bring the letter from her brother. I hoped she'd allow me to read it so I could piece together what happened.

When she arrived, she handed the letter to me.

Dear Naomi,

I wrote to a friend, Violet Colter, to enlist her help. She comes from a well-connected family. Though she and I did not part on the best of terms, she is compassionate. I am confident she will do her best to help you.

I am sorry my past continues to cause problems for you. Had I known the devastation I left behind, I would have chosen a different path. Please forgive me.

Your loving brother,

Cooper

After I read the letter, I handed it back to her.

"Do you know what he did?" I asked Naomi.

"He cheated some men out of a large sum of money. He's been hiding out in Mexico for years. Each time I write to him, he sends me a new address in his next letter."

I frowned. Clearly, he had run from his past. I had to find the letter he sent to Violet. Perhaps it explained the bizarre situation more clearly.

A few hours before the end of my workday, I left and headed over to James Colter's home. After I checked on Violet, I headed out to the shed to hunt for Forest's Bible and other papers.

After an hour, I finally found a crate full of paperwork and an envelope postmarked from Mexico. I slid the paper from the envelope and read it.

Dearest Violet,

First, let me apologize for leaving you without word. I know I hurt you, but I didn't want to. Yet, I had to. If I stayed and married you, I would have been torn from you because of my crimes. I never stopped loving you. A day doesn't go by that I don't wish I had met you before I chose the wrong path.

No wonder Forest withheld the letter. Cooper's words would only cause Violet more pain.

I hope that one day, you might forgive me. More than that, I hope you found happiness.

I know I have no right to ask this of you, but my half-sister, Naomi, needs a new job. She is leaving to start over in Prescott. My poor choices have wrecked her life as well. I pray you will receive her with compassion and help her find a position in town. Perhaps something with the railroad. She is good with accounts payable.

Again, please accept my heartfelt apology for the many ways in which I wronged you.

Cooper

"Is that it?"

At the sound of James's question, I jumped. Then I nodded.

"You cannot show her that. Forest and I agreed when I gave him the letter."

My heart raced. "You knew about this?"

James snorted as he leaned against the doorway of the shed. "It came to my home."

As I turned over the envelope, I confirmed the address was indeed his residence.

"After I read it, I gave it to Forest to let him decide how he wanted to handle it. Unfortunately, that was the day before a streetcar hit him and he passed away."

"Why didn't you tell Violet?"

James pushed away from the doorway and let his arms hang limply by his side. "I... The letter weighed on his mind. I can't help but believe if I never gave him the letter, he would not have been so distracted that he... Stepped onto the street without looking."

James cleared his throat.

"I'm responsible for that."

As my mind raced, I ran a hand through my hair. James gave Forest the letter the day before he passed. The letter from Violet's missing second beau. If Forest felt like I did, I'm certain he wrestled over what to tell Violet, just like I did now.

"You can't blame yourself," I said at last. "You can't know for certain that was what caused his death."

James shook his head. "I can. Forest was a very cautious man. He was averse to risk. It's what drew Violet to him. He was safe. Dependable. After two failed relationships, she searched for a man who would not leave her."

His shoulders slumped. "And me giving him that letter essentially took him away from her. The one man who would never leave her."

Words failed me. I wanted to assuage James's guilt, yet I doubted he'd listen. I skimmed the letter again.

"What are you going to do?"

As I folded the letter and stowed it in my jacket pocket, I sighed. "I'm not sure. I promised her I'd find the truth, not knowing what I'd find."

James nodded sullenly. "If you plan on telling her about my part in this, I'd appreciate the opportunity to tell her myself."

"Understood. Though none of that is relevant. Ultimately, she wants to know if Forest was faithful or not. The facts prove he was."

"Anyway, I should head home. I won't say anything tonight. I must pray over it," I said before I walked out the door. "Please tell her I'll stop by soon."

Then I left without waiting for James's acknowledgment.

Before I told her anything, she must recover enough to hear the news. When I told her, I needed to speak the truth gently. Tell her only what would heal the hurt in her heart and not something that would rip open old wounds.

CHAPTER 24

VIOLET

After two weeks of bed rest, the doctor finally cleared me to move around the house. He told me not to return to work at the pie shop until after the baby arrived. Being confined to James's house made me very restless.

"Morning," I greeted Zola and Katie as I escorted them in-to the parlor early in the morning. Once a week, they met me two hours before opening so we could plan for the following week.

"You look cheerful this morning," Katie said.

"I have a new recipe idea for a pot pie."

"Oh?" Zola asked.

"Broccoli cheddar."

"Hmm. That sounds good. Do you have a recipe card for the filling?"

I handed her a copy of my personal recipe. "If you're feeling adventurous, you might try a few with bacon in it."

"Any luck hiring a part-time cook?" Zola asked.

"I have a few interviews this week. I'm hoping to conduct them at the shop."

"Can't you meet with them here?" Katie asked. "We don't want you to overexert yourself."

I sighed. "I suppose I ought to. Perhaps I can ask them to bring a sample of their best dish."

"That's an excellent idea," Zola said. "If you have the inter-view in the late afternoon, I could join you."

"Yes, I don't mind closing the shop," Katie said. "I can pull the pies from the oven for you."

"Thank you both," I said as a few tears brimmed in my eyes. "You've both been wonderful."

"Thank you," Zola said. "We love working for you."

"And being independent women," Katie added.

We spent the next hour planning the pies for the week. They updated me on how close our projections were to what we sold. Then we adjusted accordingly.

"When we get closer to Thanksgiving, I want to advertise that women can order pies for the meal. We'll ask them to order ahead. But I won't be able to help bake since that's too close to my due date."

"We understand. If we hire another baker, then we should be fine," Zola said.

I smiled. She understood both the baking and the business side.

Before they left, Katie showed me the books, and I double checked her figures.

As I escorted them to the door, I said that they had every-thing under control.

"Don't you worry about anything, Violet. We'll make sure the place runs smoothly while you're gone."

That evening, Zayne finally came by after supper. I missed him, even though we spoke on the phone most evenings.

When I greeted him at the door, he smiled. "You look much improved."

"I am. Though I'll be glad when my little one arrives."

He kissed me on the cheek before I led him into the parlor.

While I told him all about the pie shop, he seemed distracted.

"I asked Zola to start a new pot pie. Peppermint chicken," I teased.

"Sounds good."

I laughed as I scooted away from him. "You would eat peppermint chicken?"

His face turned red. "I'm sorry."

"What's going on?"

He sighed. "I have a lot on my mind. So, it's not peppermint chicken?"

"No. It's broccoli cheese."

"Now that sounds good." He winked at me. "If you like broccoli."

"I do."

"Well, I won't hold it against you."

As I slid over to his side, he looped his arm around me and sighed contentedly. The more time I spent with him, the more I longed for a permanent relationship with him, despite my fears. Even though I had been left at the altar, abandoned by my second fiancé a week before my wedding, and widowed by my husband, I could dream of a future with Zayne. Him, me, Will, Eleanor, and baby Gamble.

My heart snagged. If I married Zayne, I'd have to decide if my children took his name. I frowned. It wasn't as if he asked me yet. Maybe he didn't want saddled with my two children.

Slowly, he rubbed his hands on his legs, like he often did before he left my company. I wasn't ready for him to leave.

"You've told me nothing about you or Eleanor," I said before he could announce his departure.

"I'm sorry, Violet. I have a lot on my mind."

"So you said. Won't you share it with me?"

His shoulders slumped as he angled toward me. "I don't want to cause you stress."

Just the word made me worry. "Tell me."

Zayne ran a hand through his hair. "After the baby comes, I'll tell you everything. Take it easy until then. Put the worry from your mind."

I frowned. "I'm not some delicate flower that can't handle bad news."

His eyes darted away. "You're barely recovered from the last round of bad news. I won't risk your safety or that of your baby."

He stood and held out his hands. I placed mine in his and he pulled me to my feet and into a warm embrace.

"I love you. And I'm scared for you."

As he leaned back slightly, his eyes searched mine. "I'd like to spend many years with you. So, please, don't press me on this. I promise I will explain everything when it is safe for you."

I placed my hand on his chest, then he covered it with his own. When I looked into his eyes again, I saw conflict in his soul.

"Alright. I will trust you know best." My words felt fake to me, but he really left me with no choice.

Then he brushed a soft kiss across my lips. "I'm looking forward to our future."

With that, he turned and walked out the door, leaving my heart more troubled.

Clearly, he learned something about Forest and Naomi. Or some other secret. I wished he would confide in me. If we were to marry someday, I needed complete honesty between us. No secrets. No lies. I'd suffered too much of that from my previous suitors.

CHAPTER 25

ZAYNE

Even though Violet's health improved, I would not risk her health by telling her what I uncovered about Forest, Cooper, or Naomi. She must concentrate on delivering her child.

Still, I despised myself for not telling her. It felt dishonest.

When I arrived at work the next morning, Al pulled me into his office.

"The U.S. Marshal is here."

My jaw tightened. "What does he want?"

"He wants to speak to you and Naomi. What's this about?"

I shrugged.

"He's waiting in your office."

I hurried down the hall and entered my office.

"Name's Flynn Harper," the marshal introduced himself.

After I offered him a chair, he sat.

"I'm here about Cooper James," he said as he studied my face.

When I glanced at Naomi, her face turned pale.

"What about him?" I asked.

"So, you know who he is?"

"I know he's Naomi's half-brother."

"And Violet Colter's former fiancé?" Flynn asked.

I nodded sharply.

"Why is he in Mexico?" Flynn's steely eyes locked with mine.

"I do not know. I only know that he reached out to Violet about helping Naomi."

Flynn cleared his throat as he turned his gaze on Naomi. "I've been working with James Colter regarding the money Cooper embezzled from the railway."

I coughed to mask my alarm.

"I ruled out Violet as a co-conspirator years ago. She appears never to have benefited from Cooper's theft. Also, that he left her behind shows she knew nothing about his crimes."

"Is this why those men came after me in Tucson?" Naomi asked.

"I believe so. Seems when Cooper disappeared, he took their cut of the money."

My stomach clenched over the news. I didn't like that Cooper had tried to contact Violet. If corresponding with him put Naomi in trouble, surely Violet faced danger as well.

"Ms. Fisk, when did you last hear from Cooper?"

She glanced down at her hands. "Last week."

"If you know his current whereabouts, you need to tell me," Flynn said.

I cleared my throat. "You need to tell him, Naomi. Otherwise, you could break the law. Aiding and abetting."

"That's right," Flynn said.

She looked up at me. Then she turned to face Flynn. She told him everything she knew.

"I have his most recent address hidden in my room."

Flynn leaned forward. "Would you be willing to help us bring him in?"

My heart pounded. "Are you suggesting she travel to Mexico?"

Flynn shook his head. "Ms. Fisk, I'd like you to write to him and convince him to come to Prescott. You need his help after those men found you. That you're frightened. Whatever it takes to get him on that train."

"But he's my brother. He's always been good to me."

I frowned. "Has he? It sounds like he had the means to help you financially, but he didn't."

Naomi looked at her hands for several minutes. Then she finally lifted her head and looked Flynn straight in the eyes.

"What do you want me to do?"

———

If I thought it was hard to see Violet and keep secrets from her before running into the U.S. Marshal, it was twice as hard after. I made every excuse over the next several weeks not to see her, though I called her each evening.

Two weeks after the marshal visited us, he returned to my office to meet with me and Naomi.

"My sources tell me he's headed to Yuma to catch a train," Flynn said.

"Will you arrest him there?" Naomi asked.

"No. We'll take him in when he arrives here. Too much risk of missing him along the way once he boards the train. If he comes to your home, you are to call the dry goods store. Identify yourself and ask what the going rate is for a pound of flour."

Naomi glanced away and Flynn continued, "It's important you use that wording 'going rate for a pound of flour'. Do you understand?"

"Yes, I understand."

My stomach tightened when Flynn turned his gaze to me.

"If he shows up here, call James Colter and let him know his shipment has arrived. He'll know how to contact me."

I nodded.

"It's very important both of you act as natural as possible. Cooper is a vigilant man. If he suspects anything, he'll take off and we'll lose our opportunity to bring him in."

Once the marshal left, I asked her what she told him.

Naomi glanced at the corner of the room. "Don't be mad at me. I told him... I told him Violet's husband passed, and that she was unattached."

I straightened in my chair and fisted my hand under my desk.

"I knew he wouldn't come here for me. If that was the case, he would have helped me when I lived in Tucson."

"You put her in danger," I growled.

"He won't hurt her. He loves her."

So do I.

I didn't know what I'd do if anything happened to Violet because of Naomi. As my pulse quickened, I left and headed to James's office.

When I arrived, I told him what Naomi did. James shook his head.

"That puts my entire family at risk."

"I know."

We discussed options to keep Violet and his family safe. He said he'd look into hiring some security. Despite his assurances he would keep her safe, I worried. I just hoped it would all end soon.

CHAPTER 26

October 18, 1906

VIOLET

I woke up around ten o'clock to a quiet house. After I groomed for the day, I left my hair loose around my shoulders. My swollen feet no longer fit in my shoes, so I wore a pair of slippers. My dress stretched taut across my middle. I held a hand below my belly as I descended the stairs.

Once at the bottom of the stairs, I sat in the chair by the phone. James had placed one of the dining room chairs there for me. I often rested before climbing the stairs. I also sat there while Zayne and I talked on the phone.

The doctor visited me yesterday and thought I still had three to four weeks left until my baby arrived. Four weeks sounded like an eternity.

When I sat in the chair, I saw the note from Keri. She took the children on an outing to the park, along with one of the security guards. James hadn't explained the sudden need for security. I sighed as I rested in the chair. Secrets swirled around me. No one wanted me to go into labor too early, so they told me nothing. They didn't realize that not knowing stressed me too.

When the phone rang, I jumped.

"Hello?" I answered.

"Vi? It's Mama. How are you feeling today?"

I sniffed to hold back the tears. "Like a giant, lumbering ox."

Mama's laughter floated across the line to my ear. "I think you're closer to the due date than the doctor realizes."

I snorted. "When I carried Will, it was so different. I feel gigantic. And sore. And I just woke up a little while ago."

"I know, sweetheart. Soon enough, you'll have your baby in your arms and forget all about this. Rest as much as you need to."

"Thanks Mama."

"Do you want me to stop by tomorrow?"

"Only if you're in town. Don't make a special trip for me."

"Alright. Take it easy. I love you, Vi."

As soon as I ended the call, I had a craving for one of my chocolate cream pies. It was strange. I hadn't eaten breakfast yet, and I already wanted dessert.

I picked up the phone again.

"Zayne?"

"Violet." I heard the warm smile in his voice.

"Are you busy? Would you like to eat lunch here?"

The line went silent for a moment.

"In a half hour?" he asked.

"That would be lovely. And can you ask Zola for one of my chocolate cream pies?"

He laughed. "Of course. See you soon."

After hanging up the earpiece, I waddled into the dining room. I asked Maria to fix sandwiches for me and Zayne. Ten minutes later, Maria backed into the room. Then I saw him.

"Cooper." My stomach clenched and my throat went dry.

"Violet."

The angry frown disappeared from his face as those green eyes roamed over my face, hair, and dress.

"What are you doing here?" I asked before I folded my shaky hands on my belly and remained seated.

"That your late husband's?" He nodded to my protruding belly.

"What do you think?" I failed to keep the acid from my voice.

After six long years, he had some nerve showing up at my brother's house uninvited.

"Sit," he commanded Maria.

I glanced at the front door. *Please hurry, Zayne.*

"Don't worry, Vi. I only knocked him out."

The blood drained from my face and my breathing shallowed.

"You seem awful surprised to see me. Yet a man guards the place."

Cooper's eyes shot daggers my direction as he eased into a chair across from me.

"What are you doing here?" I asked again as a sharp pain tightened across my lower abdomen. I groaned as I leaned forward.

"Mrs. Gamble here," Maria said as she held a glass of water for me. After I took a few small sips, she stroked my back and whispered to me to breathe slowly.

"I came for you," Cooper said.

I snorted. "You're about six years too late for that."

"Didn't you get my letter?" he asked.

"What letter?"

He frowned. "I apologized. I told you I still love you."

"Ha! Love does not abandon—"

"Violet?" Zayne's voice preceded him.

Cooper shot to his feet. "Who's that?"

"Zayne!" I yelled. "Help!"

Cooper pointed his gun at me. "Quiet!"

I narrowed my eyes. "You would really shoot a pregnant woman? Have you gone mad?"

He lowered the weapon and set it on the table as Zayne entered the room.

"Violet," Zayne said as his eyes remained fixed on Cooper. "Are you alright?"

"I'm." I groaned. "Fine."

His head snapped my direction as he set a chocolate cream pie on the table.

When he took a step toward me, Cooper snatched up the gun and pointed it at Zayne.

"Don't!" I yelled and tears streamed down my face.

Cooper narrowed his eyes at me. "You didn't waste any time finding your next man, did you?" He spat out the words as if they had left a bitter taste in his mouth.

"Cooper, I presume?" Zayne asked as he slid closer to me.

"Zayne."

"What's your end game here?" Zayne asked. "From everything James told me, you are only wanted for embezzlement. Not murder."

"Embezzlement? What does James know?" I asked.

Zayne shook his head at me.

"What is going on?" I asked.

Another sharp pain hit me and stole my breath. Zayne slid into the chair beside me before he turned his attention to me, ignoring Cooper.

"Did the pains just start?"

I nodded as another ripped into me. When it subsided, my body relaxed against the back of the chair.

"I. Need to. Lay down."

Exhaustion pulled at me. I wanted to close my eyes, but I needed to get back upstairs first.

"Let me take her upstairs," Zayne said.

Cooper frowned but nodded after a moment.

As he led me up the stairs, he whispered to me, "Is there another phone besides the one in the hall?"

"James's office."

By the time we reached the top of the stairs, I huffed. Slowly, with Cooper watching from the bottom of the stairs, Zayne helped me to my room.

After I rested in bed, he turned away. I grabbed his arm and dug my nails into it. "Please, don't leave me."

"Zayne!" Cooper's voice sounded angrier than I'd ever heard before.

I yelled loudly as another pain tore at my stomach.

The last thing I saw before I closed my eyes was the fear in Zayne's.

CHAPTER 27

ZAYNE

When I walked into the dining room to see Cooper James pointing a gun at Violet, my stomach clenched. I needed to get her out of there. But how?

We exchanged some words until Violet moaned in pain. Helping her to bed quickly became my priority. As soon as I had her settled and she passed out, I walked down the stairs. I had to get Cooper out of the house or get a message to the marshal.

I glanced toward James's study.

"Don't think about it," Cooper said as he waved the gun at me. "Dining room is the perfect room for a chat."

My mind raced through a dozen possibilities. If Cooper killed me, Eleanor would have no parents. Even though I knew my family would care for her, the thought kept me from doing anything risky. Keeping myself safe was as important as keeping Violet from danger.

I shot a prayer heavenward as I sat in my seat again. The second hand on the clock ticked. With each click, my anxiety rose.

"Cooper?" Naomi's voice came from the kitchen.

I straightened in my chair as she entered the room.

"I received your message. Why did you come here?" she asked.

"I came for Violet."

She snorted. "Not to help me?"

He frowned. "You can come too."

"Why don't you put the gun down?" Her eyes darted to me when she said it.

Just as I figured out her stare was a message, Marshal Harper entered the room. Cooper turned his gun on him, but Flynn knocked the weapon to the ground before I blinked. Then he shoved Cooper up against the wall.

"You're under arrest," Flynn said. Then he secured his hands with shackles.

I finally let out the breath I'd been holding.

Violet screamed from her room, and I looked at Flynn. He nodded, and I darted to my feet.

In a matter of minutes, I arrived by her side. "I'm here. I'm right here, Violet."

Tears streamed down her face and sweat beaded her forehead, matting the edges of her dark hair against her face. The scene felt all too familiar. Pale skin. Quick breaths. Fear.

A minute later, Maria joined us. She brought a cool cloth and mopped it on Violet's brow.

"The doctor is on his way. The marshal is gone with his prisoner and so is the young woman."

I took the cloth from Maria's hand.

"Call her brother and her mother. Let them know to come quickly."

Maria left the room and did as I asked.

"Zayne." Violet's voice sounded weak. "Something is wrong. Very wrong."

A sob caught in her throat.

"Shh. Everything is fine. It's probably false contractions

like last time. Relax."

"I. Can't lose. His child."

Tears burned my eyes. I couldn't lose her or her child. My heart wouldn't survive the loss.

I cleared my throat. "When you deliver this baby and are healthy again, I'm going to marry you. You hear me?"

"I'd. Like. That."

Her eyes fluttered shut.

My heart lodged in my throat as unformed words tore from my heart heavenward.

Noise sounded from downstairs. Then the doctor appeared, and I moved aside as he examined her. I don't know when Keri arrived, but she dragged me from the room.

James suggested I sit in the parlor. I stared numbly into the fire.

Please, Lord, keep her and the baby safe. The words repeated in my heart as I begged for her life.

It seemed like years before the doctor came downstairs.

"She's exhausted, but she's not in labor. It's important she remains in bed until the baby comes naturally. Weeks, if that is what it takes. Absolutely no stress. Otherwise, I'm not sure the baby will make it."

A strangled sound came from my throat. It would kill her to lose Forest's child.

"Zayne," James said. "Let my driver take you home."

Numbly, I allowed him to usher me from his house.

"We'll call if anything changes."

I thought about the strange turn of events as I slid into the car. Here I was, a widower, rooting for the woman I wanted to marry not to lose her dead husband's child. All this after her former fiancé tried to kidnap her. The man was my employee's half-brother. As I climbed the porch stairs to my home, I shook my head. I didn't think I could explain it to my mother.

When she greeted me, I told her Violet was on bedrest for the duration of her pregnancy. Then I went to my room to pray for the woman I loved.

CHAPTER 28

November 6, 1906

VIOLET

Before the sun rose, I woke up to a fiercely aching back. I shimmied to the edge of the bed and sat up.

"Vi?" Mama's voice came from the dark.

Despite my relief she stayed with me, I still felt guilty that my sixty-four-year-old mother slept on a cot wedged between my bed and the wardrobe.

"Is it time?"

The cot squeaked as she climbed out of it. Then she lit a lamp.

"Oh, don't stand," she said.

"I need to move."

She sighed and helped me to my feet. We walked a few paces to the hall. Then I shuffled my feet before we turned around. We repeated the process several times. Then my water broke and Mama led me back to my bed.

The birthing pains muddled my mind. Time sped up and stood still. I concentrated on bringing my child into this world. Between panting and yelling, I sent prayers heavenward for his safe arrival.

Then my squirming son rested in my arms. Tears trailed down my cheeks as Keri mopped my face.

"Forest," I whispered, "you'll have to wait a long time to meet your son. But one day you will. I'm sorry another man will raise him."

I kissed my son's forehead before I offered him the meal he craved.

"Owen Forest Gamble. Wear your father's name with pride."

When he finished, Mama took him and laid him in the bassinet.

"Tell Zayne," I asked Keri. "Let him know I'm fine."

"I will. Rest now."

The next few days blurred as I knew they would. Feedings. Sleep. Rest for Owen. Rest for me.

A week. Then two. I finally felt up to seeing Zayne.

As I donned a loose-fitting dress, I left my hair down. I knew so many of my interactions with Zayne would have scandalized society, so choosing comfort came easy. He would be my husband soon enough. I had no doubts.

With Owen cradled in my arms, I eased my way down the stairs. Then I sat in the parlor and waited for the man who stole my heart so many months ago.

I smiled as I remembered the look of desperation on his face the first day he showed up in my pie shop. Who knew that one simple act of kindness from me would lead to an act of kindness from him?

"Hello there." Zayne's soft voice drew my gaze.

When I smiled at him, the worry faded from his features. Love, deep and abiding, replaced it.

"Come meet him." I almost invited him to see his son. Owen wasn't his. Not yet.

Zayne sat next to me and looped an arm around my

shoulders. He burrowed his nose in my hair and inhaled deeply. When he let it out, I heard the shakiness of it before his lips brushed my forehead.

"I'm fine. Better than fine," I whispered.

"I needed to see for myself."

I glanced at him before I introduced my son. "Owen Forest Gamble, I want you to meet Zayne Harrison. You'll be seeing a lot of him."

My heart wanted to speak more. I wanted to promise my son that Zayne would always be there for him. That he'd love him like his own. I knew it to be true deep in my heart.

There was only one significant problem: Zayne had yet to propose. I didn't want to pressure him. He needed to decide how and when he asked.

When he did, I would agree.

———

ZAYNE

Relief flooded me from my brow to my toes when I saw Violet smiling. Rose tinged her cheeks. Her eyes sparkled as she gazed down at her son.

My heart ached. How I wanted to claim him as my son. With one look into the blue eyes matching his mother's, I loved him. He shared her dark hair, too.

"Hello Owen Forest Gamble."

My voice sounded strange as feelings stronger than I would have guessed possible washed over me. Love. Protectiveness. Pride. Joy. I wondered if that was how my papa felt when he brought home each of my siblings, none of which were his own blood. My heart made a silent promise to Owen to treat him like my own, and to teach him about his father. He deserved that.

"Do you want to hold him?" Violet asked.

"Of course."

She shifted so I could cradle his head in my overly large hand. He seemed so tiny. Smaller than I remembered Eleanor.

"He's perfect. And he looks just like you."

Her laughter warmed me.

I grinned at him before I turned my gaze to her. Her smile faded.

"Would you mind putting him in the bassinet? We are long overdue for a conversation."

I did as she asked. Then I braced myself for the questions I knew she waited weeks to ask.

CHAPTER 29

VIOLET

Thankfully, the nanny occupied Will while Keri hid out in James's office, giving Zayne and I some much needed privacy. My mind filled with a dozen questions. Where to start?

"Tell me why Forest had Naomi's picture."

Zayne shifted to look me in the eye. "Cooper had written a letter to you, asking for your help on Naomi's behalf. It arrived in April."

I frowned as my pulse quickened.

"Forest withheld the letter from you. Cooper had no right to say those things."

Zayne glanced away. "Had I intercepted a letter like that to my wife…" His gazed connected with mine. "I would have burned it and taken its existence to my grave."

Slowly, I nodded. I understood what he didn't say. Cooper confessed his undying love for me like he had before Zayne arrived on the scene.

"Forest was faithful to me then?"

He nodded. "Completely."

My shoulders sagged as I blew out a loud breath.

"Cooper wanted you to help Naomi get a job. As you know, she managed fine on her own."

"So, how did he end up here?" I asked, still lost about how events connected.

"U.S. Marshal Flynn Harper has been tracking him for years. When James learned about the letter—"

"James knew about the letter?" I sat up straighter.

"Forest must have mentioned it to him. Anyway, James had been working with Flynn about Cooper's crimes. Flynn enlisted Naomi's help to lure Cooper to town."

He reached out and took my hand. "I'm sorry. She used you as the lure. I never would have allowed that."

I squeezed his hand.

"None of us knew exactly when he'd arrive. Once I found out that Naomi mentioned you, I told James. And thus, the reason for the security guards."

I snorted. They had done little to help.

Zayne ran a hand through his hair. "That's it. You know what happened to Cooper."

"Not exactly. Is he going to jail?" I asked. Not that I cared overly much.

"Yes. They shipped him off to the territorial prison in Yuma. It's unlikely we'll ever see him again."

"And Naomi?"

"She's very sorry for involving you and that her brother brought trouble to your doorstep."

I didn't say a word as I tried to absorb the news. Then one detail hit me hard.

"April. You said Forest received the letter in April?"

Zayne looked away and nodded.

"What aren't you telling me?" I asked as my heart squeezed tight.

He cleared his throat. "James thinks that the news may have led to..."

My vision blurred as the grief buried me. "The accident."

"I'm so sorry, Violet."

As sobs shook my body, he pulled me into his arms. I rested my head against his chest. My hands clutched his shirt tightly until the sorrow subsided.

Even though I desired to stay in his embrace longer, Owen fussed. I stood and dried my face with my handkerchief. Then I lifted Owen into my arms.

"I need to…"

I hurried from the room to the kitchen, where I nursed my son. I lingered there for a moment, hesitant to return to Zayne.

Such a tangled mess. Cooper, the man who disappeared without a trace, set off a chain of events that led to Forest's death. I wondered how I could have been so utterly fooled by Cooper back then.

The tears came again. Forest lost his life because of my past. I was the reason our marriage ended far too early and robbed us of our lifetime together.

Yet, Forest was gone. My heart longed for a new man. A man who I desperately prayed would share a lifetime with me.

———

ZAYNE

When Violet failed to return to the parlor, I stood outside the kitchen door and listened. Soft sobs came from the other side.

My heart broke. I promised her I would tell her the painful news. And her heart shattered.

I turned and left.

When I arrived home, I sat on the porch sipping a coffee.

The cool air pricked my skin. I didn't care. The fresh air soothed my guilt. I should never have made that promise.

After a while, Mama joined me. I told her everything. All the horrible details.

"You did the right thing. She deserved to know the truth."

"Then why do I feel so terrible?"

Mama patted my arm. "Because you care for her."

I stared at the tall oak tree on the corner of the property. "How long should I wait before I marry her?"

Mama sighed. "I think that's a question you need to pray about. I don't have an answer for you."

When she shivered, she made her excuses and returned inside. I sat there for several minutes more, praying and thinking. Ideas took shape, and I knew the way forward.

CHAPTER 30

December 7, 1906

VIOLET

Midafternoon in early December, Zola stopped by the house to tell me about the pie shop. The new baker, Janet Richardson, lived up to her claims. Zola took over managing the shop, while Janet became the primary baker. Katie manned the front desk and the ledgers. The shop continued to grow.

I wrote new recipes and left it up to Zola to turn them into masterpieces. When I dreamed of the future of the shop, I knew I'd continue to contribute recipes. But I was also content to allow my employees to keep it all running. I didn't plan to return to the shop in the same capacity as before Owen was born.

"Zayne is here," Keri announced. "He wondered if you might meet him in the dining room."

I reached for Owen, but Keri stopped me. "If he wakes up, I'll bring him to you."

"Alright."

When I walked into the dining room, my breath caught.

Candlelight cast a warm glow on Zayne's handsome face. His blue-gray eyes sparkled with life. Flowers stood in a vase, lending an ethereal feeling to the ambiance. He held a chair out for me. After I sat, he kneeled in front of me.

"Violet, I have loved you for as long as I can remember."

He chuckled.

"Though my love has matured, just as I have. We have both suffered tremendous losses. Yet neither of us closed off our hearts to love. And I'm glad, because what blossomed between us is truly special."

He held out a piece of apple pie. "You recaptured my heart that day in the pie shop. One slice of apple pie, a dirty diaper, and your beautiful smile. From that moment onward, my heart was yours."

"I'm pretty sure you ate two slices of pie that day."

He grinned. "You got me."

I raised my eyebrow, wanting him to continue.

"Will you marry me, Violet Colter-Gamble?"

"Yes."

He set the slice of pie on the table. Then he took my hand and slid a ring on my finger before he stood, and he pulled me into his arms.

As I slid my arms behind his neck, he lowered his lips to mine. Mmm. He tasted like apple pie. The scoundrel already ate a piece.

The thought fled as his lips caressed mine warmly. I pressed closer when his hands roamed over my back. Love for him welled up from my soul.

When he ended the kiss, I leaned back, glad I broke my promise to myself. Glad I opened my heart to love again.

"Just one more question for you," Zayne said, as a grin spread across his lips. "Are you gonna eat that piece of pie?"

I laughed. "You can have it. I know where to find more."

———

ZAYNE

By the end of supper, we agreed to an early February date. Owen would be three months old. By that time, Violet thought he should sleep through the night.

I would have been happy to marry her tomorrow, despite the challenges of a newborn. But I knew she wanted our wedding day to focus on us and not our children. Compared to a lifetime with her, two more months seemed a small sacrifice.

During that time, I readied a nursery in my home. I placed a second crib in the room at the end of the hall. Neither Violet nor I thought we should take Eleanor out of her crib until closer to her second birthday.

The months of waiting seemed to stretch as I longed to welcome Violet, Will, and Owen into our home.

In January, Jedediah and Mama moved out of the house and into his house next door. His renters left in late December. Then Miss Harmony, Mama, and some of my sisters cleaned up the place. Over one very long, exhausting weekend, we moved their things into their new home and moved my things down to the master suite.

The following weekend, the Colter men and Grady moved all Violet's things out of James's shed and into our home. As more of her things arrived, my house felt like ours. I longed for her to join me.

Since she had no energy left after caring for Owen, I spent very little time with her. Sometimes I went over to James's house to pick up Will for a walk with me and Eleanor. Other times, Violet and I just chatted on the phone.

We moved the last of her things to our room before our wedding. She kept only a few changes of clothing for her and Will at James's house. And the things to care for a newborn.

As I crawled into bed the night before our wedding, I sighed contentedly. Tomorrow, the woman I loved for more than half my life would finally become my wife.

CHAPTER 31

February 9, 1907

ZAYNE

My entire family filled one side of the church as I stood at the front. Violet's family filled the other side. When my gaze drifted to Mama and Jedediah, she smiled. I remembered our conversation from a few weeks after I moved back to Prescott. She told me I would find love again. Little did I know it would happen so quickly.

As I shifted my feet, Al squeezed my shoulder. "Relax. She's here."

Boone made his way up the side aisle, and I frowned. He motioned for me. My stomach knotted as I approached.

"Owen just woke up. She was ready to leave, but it will take a while."

I sighed and returned to my place at the front of the church.

"Papa!" Eleanor giggled.

"Zay!" Will squirmed and broke free from his aunt's grasp. He ran up the aisle and hugged my knee.

I kneeled down to his level. Then I tweaked his nose. "Go

sit with Aunt Keri."

His eyes held my gaze. "You my papa now?"

I chuckled as I understood his confusion. Violet and I told him after she and I stood at the front of the church together, I would be his papa. Guess he forgot about the part that she would stand across from me.

"Not yet. Soon."

"K."

He blazed down the aisle and sat next to Keri.

The music started, and my gaze darted to the back. Will Colter stood with a frown on his face. He took off his tan cowboy hat and ran a hand through his hair. Then he plopped it back down on his head. He gestured towards someone and grabbed an arm. Slowly, Violet came into view.

Her hand shook as she patted her hair. Red colored her cheeks as he placed her hand in the crook of his arm. The red faded as they took one step. Then another.

When her eyes met mine, my heart nearly burst. My resilient bride looked stunning. Her smile faltered and moisture gathered in the corners of her eyes. Her inner strength might not be visible to everyone, but it was to me. I felt honored that she'd risk her heart yet again just for me.

At last, she stood next to me and her father stepped back.

"You showed up," she whispered.

I took her hand, even though I wasn't supposed to yet. "I promised I would."

Her eyes darted away.

"Are you ready?" I asked.

She nodded slowly.

I nodded to the pastor to begin.

My gaze never left hers as we said our vows. Tears gathered in her eyes when she choked out the words "death do us part." I wished I could promise her we'd share decades together. We discussed our hurt over having fewer years than we expected with our first spouses. We would cherish every year with each other and trust that God would give us a long marriage.

When the pastor told me I could kiss my wife, I smiled. Then I planted a big kiss on her lips just as Owen cried. Will ran up the aisle and grabbed my leg as Eleanor belted out a loud, "Mama!"

I released my wife and laughed. "Guess our kissing is over."

Violet gave me a saucy grin. "For now."

As I clasped her hand in mine, she took Will's hand in hers and the three of us walked down the aisle together. We went to the fellowship hall for the reception.

After a while, Miss Harmony collected the children and took them home. We followed behind, eager for some stolen moments alone.

When we entered the house, Miss Harmony promised to get Owen to take a bottle. I hoped he would. Violet said he'd refused to. I really wanted just one night alone with my wife.

Once the children settled with Miss Harmony upstairs, I carried my bride across the threshold of the downstairs bedroom. I was grateful for the large, secluded room.

"It's lovely," Violet whispered.

I paid no attention to the room. Only to my lovely wife as I ran my fingers through her hair, pulling each hair pin from her silky dark locks. She fiddled with the top few buttons on my shirt before she paused.

"I've changed my mind."

My hand froze, and my throat tightened. "A little late for that."

She giggled. "Not about that."

I quirked an eyebrow and held my breath until she continued unbuttoning my shirt.

"I think you are dashing. Quite so."

A loud breath left my lungs.

"Why? What did you think I meant?" Her coy smile told me she intended to give me a little fright.

"You." I groaned.

"Did you really think I wouldn't tease you back after all those pranks?"

As I tossed the hairpins on the dresser, I tasted her sweet lips, stopping her from any further teasing. Then we celebrated our wedding night.

———

VIOLET

The next morning, I woke feeling more rested than I had in months. Zayne's arm rested lightly over my stomach. I snuggled closer, so glad I had opened my heart to him and that I saw him for the man he had become and not that rascal from school. I reached up and brushed his sandy brown hair back from his eyes.

"Mmm." He moaned before his blue-gray eyes popped open. "I do like waking up next to you, wife."

In the distance, I heard Owen's cries. I sighed and threw back the covers. Zayne's arm tightened around me.

"Let him cry for a few minutes. Miss Harmony will see to him."

I bit my lip.

"Mrs. Harrison," he said, "you now have help with the children."

As I relaxed, he scooted closer and started kissing my neck.

Little shivers ran down my arms.

"Good thing too. Because I plan on filling all those rooms upstairs."

"I don't know. With how nervous you were before Owen arrived, I'm not sure I can stand it," I said.

He stopped kissing my neck and looked into my eyes. "I promise to trust your safety to God. I know I am helpless to protect you, even though I yearn to."

As I turned onto my side, I scooted closer and ran my fingers through his hair.

"That sounds like a good idea."

Just as he kissed me again, the door flew open. Zayne groaned and yanked the sheets up to my neck right before Will jumped on the bed.

"Papa! Mama! I'm hungry."

I laughed as my heart warmed over my son's complete acceptance of his new father. When he was older, we would teach him about Forest and why he carried a different name from his siblings.

Zayne grabbed him by the waist and pointed him to the door. Then he tapped his rear. "Out squirt. Give us a few minutes."

Will pouted but hurried out of the room as Zayne reached for his trousers. He stood and closed the door so I could get dressed.

"Do you believe we did the right thing?" I asked.

"Leaving his name Gamble?"

I nodded.

"He might have some memories of him, so I think it's fair."

We had decided Owen would carry the Harrison name and use Gamble as one of his two middle names, since Owen would only know Zayne as his father. It was how we honored both Forest and Zayne.

"Come on. We'd better get out there before Ella figures out how to open this door and comes barging in."

"I think you should put a lock on it," I suggested.

"Excellent idea, wife."

I giggled. "Thank you, husband."

After I donned my nightgown and robe, the two of us joined our three children for our first meal as a family. My heart overflowed with joy and love for each face that graced my table.

EPILOGUE

Colter Ranch
November 30, 1922

VIOLET

On Thanksgiving day, we hosted an enormous meal for the Colters and Harrisons at the lodge on the ranch. I smiled as Zayne helped me from the automobile. He held on to my hand for a few breaths longer. Fifteen years and I loved him more than I imagined possible.

"Will, Owen, help your sisters out," I said as I exited the automobile. I placed my hand on Zayne's arm.

Both boys would do as they were told. Sure enough, Eleanor, Vivian, and Maxine hurried past us to greet their cousins.

"How many were we expecting?" I asked.

"Sixty something on the Harrison side," Zayne answered.

"I suppose we are close to that on the Colter side, too."

When I saw Mama hobble toward the lodge, I left Zayne and hurried to catch up to her. A twinge of sadness pierced my heart. She turned eighty that year. Papa had passed several years before, leaving Mama alone. Though not really. Sterling and his wife added a first-floor room and private washroom onto the ranch house for her. Despite my many attempts to convince her to move to town, Mama would hear nothing of it. Colter Ranch would be her home until the good Lord called her to heaven.

"Vi!" She greeted me with a kiss on the cheek. "It is wonderful to let a new generation take over cooking."

I laughed. "You mean to tell me you didn't help at all? Not even with a single pie?"

Mama laughed. "That wife of Sterling's has an eagle eye. Wouldn't let me near the stove."

"Good. You have earned a break from cooking family meals."

As I helped her into the lodge, her breath caught. "Are there so many of us?"

"Yes, Mama. Between the Colters and Harrisons alone, we're nearly one hundred. When you add in the Thatchers, Glassmans, and Harpers, well, there's a lot of us."

"Mama!" Boone hollered from across the room.

His oldest son, Jaxson, ran over and lifted Mama off her feet as he twirled her around.

"Put your grandmother down," Jaclyn scolded him. I guess one was never too old to be scolded by his mother.

Mama's cheeks turned pink as he set her back down before he led her to the head of the table. Zayne's mother, Grace, sat at the head of another table. The two matriarchs beamed as they greeted children, grandchildren, and even some great-grandchildren.

My heart warmed as each of my children greeted Mama and then Grace.

James rang the dinner bell, and the room silenced except for a few rowdy children or crying babies. As had become our tradition, he offered a prayer for the family members who passed on. Papa. Zayne's father, Joshua, and his stepfather,

Jedediah. Some of his brothers. Some of our nephews lost in the Great War.

Then he prayed over the meal. As soon as the "amens" echoed throughout the lodge, the clatter of platters and silverware sounded. Each table began sharing what they were thankful for.

Zayne leaned over and trailed his fingers along my cheek. "You know it's you, yet again."

I laughed. "What? And not my pie?"

"The pie is a close second."

"I'm thankful for this extensive family," I said. "Sometimes I wonder if Papa dreamed so many of his relatives would fill the ranch when he first settled on the land."

"I'm sure he never expected the Harrisons to be counted among his relatives."

"Oh?"

Zayne smiled. "Mama recently told me that my father was once sweet on your mother. But your father captured her heart instead."

I nearly choked on the news.

"Turns out your father never really warmed up to mine."

I narrowed my eyes at my husband. "Is this one of your pranks?"

He shook his head. "You can ask your mama or mine."

"Who would have guessed?"

The meal continued on, just like every Thanksgiving celebrated on the ranch. Smiles and laughter. Love and faith bound the family together, leaving a legacy for generations to come.

Author's Note

When I first mapped out the Colter Sons Series, I intended to write only about the five sons. Yet, as Violet's character developed over the course of those five books, the series felt incomplete to me without telling her story. I wrote most of it before I started writing Preston's story, and I originally planned to release it as a standalone novel.

With so many hints about Zayne Harrison throughout the series, I knew the only satisfying end to Violet's story had to include him. But they needed time to mature and grow before they were ready for their love match.

The idea of Violet's complicated back story with three suitors, with only one making it to the altar, took shape. Once I opened the story with Forest's funeral and made Zayne a widower and single father, I knew Violet carrying Forest's child provided the extra tension needed for Zayne's character to grow.

Though the historical events took a distant backseat to Violet and Zayne's story, I included several historically relevant details. After a trip to Prescott last summer, I picked up a copy of Bradley G. Courtney's book, *The Whiskey Row Fire of 1900*. I originally considered killing off Cooper James in the great fire, but after reading Courtney's book and learning no one died, I wanted to stay true to history. So, the great fire ended up being the perfect cover for Cooper to skip town.

This past year, I also joined a Facebook group run by several historians about Prescott's history. It's been fun learning even more about the town's history. One member posted a photo and article about the streetcar in Prescott, which started operation in 1905 and ceased operation in 1912. So, Prescott really had a streetcar, though I have no evidence that anyone was injured in any accidents.

The Facebook group also helped me nail down the dates of the first phones used in Prescott. We figured they were widely available when the first exchange was installed in 1902, though the SFP&P installed some lines between their stations in 1894, those weren't public lines.

As the Colter Sons Series closes, I hope you enjoyed reading the stories of the second generation Colters. Don't be surprised if future generations share their own stories, though it may be a while.

If you enjoyed the Colter Sons Series, try my contemporary Christian cowboy romance Vargas Ranch Series starting with Falling for a Real Cowboy (Vargas Ranch Book 1).

Thank you, readers, for your continued support and encouragement. May God bring a smile to your face at the end of each story.

Karen Baney

Want More Arizona Territory Romance?

Get a FREE novella featuring characters connected to the Colter Sons series! Plus exclusive updates on new releases, special offers, and historical insights from the frontier.

Subscribe at: books.karenbaney.com/larson-christmas

ABOUT THE AUTHOR

Karen Baney is passionate about writing stories full of flawed characters. She enjoys weaving together stories of second chances, redemption, and overcoming personal trials. As a transplant to Arizona, she loves researching the state's history and finding ways to seamlessly incorporate real history and real settings into her novels. In addition to writing and speaking, Karen works as a Software Development Manager for a Christian ministry.

Her faith plays an important role both in her life and in her writing. Karen and her husband, Jim, make their home in Gilbert, Arizona, with their two dogs, Bella and Daisy. Both Jim and Karen are active at Rock Point Church in Queen Creek, Arizona.

Discover faith-laced stories with characters who feel like lifelong friends.

Visit www.karenbaney.com to discover more historical romance series set in the American West. Follow Karen's writing journey and get behind-the-scenes glimpses of her research adventures on social media.

Facebook:	@AuthorKarenBaney
X:	@karen_baney
Instagram:	@AuthorKarenBaney
BookBub:	Follow Karen Baney for new release alerts

BOOKS BY KAREN BANEY

Historical Western Romance

Prescott Pioneers Series:

Step back in time to the wild, untamed Arizona Territory where survival depends on grit, faith, and the courage to start over. Follow three pioneer families—the Andersons, Colters, and Larsons—as they risk everything for the promise of a new life in a land that demands both strength and hope.

A Dream Unfolding
A Heart Renewed
A Life Restored
A Hope Revealed
Hidden Prospects

Desert Manna Series:

Sometimes the most beautiful love stories bloom in the desert. Set in the growing frontier town of Prescott during the early 1870s, these tender romances follow women rebuilding their lives after heartbreak and the unexpected men who help them discover that second chances at love are worth the risk. Set in Prescott, Arizona between 1871 - 1873.

Beauty for Ashes
Joy for Mourning
Oaks of Justice

Colter Sons Series:

Power, legacy, and forbidden love collide in this sweeping family saga set in the Arizona Territory. The Colter ranch empire has weathered decades of frontier life, but now family secrets and buried betrayals threaten to destroy everything. As five brothers—and one resilient sister—navigate the treacherous waters of love, loss, and redemption, they must decide what's worth fighting for. Set in Prescott and other locations within the Arizona Territory in 1887 - 1906.

The Reluctant Cattleman
The Roaming Adventurer
The Railroad Magnate
The Resourceful Stockman
The Restless Wrangler
The Resilient Bride

Larson Sisters Series
Meet the next generation! These delightful novellas follow the three daughters of Adam and Julia Larson from the *Prescott Pioneers Series* as they navigate love, courtship, and finding their own happily ever afters in territorial Arizona in 1886 – 1894.

In Love at Christmas
In Love with the Rancher
In Love with the Horse Trainer

Contemporary Romance

Vargas Ranch Series:
Love is in the air at the Vargas Guest Ranch & Resort near Wickenburg, Arizona. Meet the Vargas family—five swoonworthy brothers and their cousins who live by their family motto: "We do not deviate from the Lord's plan." These rugged cowboys run a successful working ranch and luxury re-

sort while navigating the rollercoaster of finding true love.

Falling for a Fake Cowboy
Falling for a Real Cowboy
Honeymoon with a Real Cowboy
Falling for a Shy Cowboy
Falling for a Bossy Cowboy
Falling for a Smart Cowboy
Falling for a Humbug Cowboy
Falling for a Devoted Cowgirl
Falling for a Pregnant Cowgirl
Falling for a Cowboy's Legacy

Steadfast Love Series:

The *Steadfast Love* series follows a close-knit group of friends as they navigate the beautiful mess of modern life in the Phoenix area—workplace drama, complicated families, and love that shows up when they least expect it. These contemporary romances blend emotional depth with authentic faith, reminding us that even when life unravels, God's love never does.

The Heart I Rescue (prequel)
The Air I Breathe

Family Drama Contemporary Cowboy Romance

We do not deviate from the Lord's plan.
--Vargas Family Motto

DISCOVER THE VARGAS RANCH SERIES

Love is in the air at the Vargas Guest Ranch & Resort near Wickenburg, Arizona. Meet the Vargas family—five swoon-worthy brothers and their cousins who live by their family motto: "We do not deviate from the Lord's plan." These rugged cowboys run a successful working ranch and luxury resort while navigating the rollercoaster of finding true love.

Will this city-meets-country duo find love where they least expect it?

She's trying to resurrect her career. He's sworn off women.

Dalton J. Vargas the fourth has sworn off love. Women are just a distraction that keep him from running his family's multi-million-dollar guest ranch near Wickenburg, Arizona. After his father announces an early retirement, the full burden of the ranch rests on his shoulders. When a city-slicker romance author stays at the ranch, Dalton's perfect world turns to chaos.

River Sloane's last workplace romance novel flopped—big time. Now her publisher wants her to write a modern-day cowboy romance, which she has resisted for years. When her publisher sends her to a dude ranch in the middle of nowhere Arizona, she must learn about cowboys and ranching to get her career back on track. One hunky cowboy stirs her heart and unexpectedly becomes her muse.

Will she let herself fall in love with the real cowboy or will she return to the life she left behind? Will Dalton open his heart to a new, lasting love?

DESERT LIFE MEDIA

Desert Life Media: *There Is Life in The Desert*

Entertainment–first Christian fiction set in the Southwest, featuring redemption, family, and faith

Publishing clean, wholesome, and uplifting fiction since 2010

---

desertlifemedia.com

www.ingramcontent.com/pod-product-compliance
Lightning Source LLC
Chambersburg PA
CBHW051946220626
47052CB00004B/814